BEST IN BREED

A LOCUST POINT COZY MYSTERY

LIBBY HOWARD

CHAPTER 1

$\mathcal{I}$ reached up to turn on the outdoor heater, the wooden porch chair I was standing on wobbling under my feet.

"Kay! For Pete's sake!" Strong hands gripped my waist, steadying me. "I could have gotten that," Judge Beck scolded.

The heater flared to life with a blaze. I stepped down, grateful for the judge's help as I descended.

"Thanks." I smiled up at him. "I didn't realize that thing was so rickety."

He let go of my waist to pick the chair up. "I'll take it around back so no one sits on it. Henry can fix it when he's back on Sunday."

The boy had become quite the handyman. I'd taken to assigning him various tasks around the house and paying him small sums for his repair work. So far he'd patched the drywall where several years ago a door handle had punched a hole, changed the light bulbs on the porch and other outdoor fixtures. He'd replaced the cracked glass in a display cabinet, and replaced some chipped tile in one of the upstairs bathrooms. I had every confidence that this chair would be good as new under his skilled hands.

While the judge took the chair around to the back porch, I set out the wine and the glasses, then went inside to get the charcuterie platters from the kitchen. We were expecting a full house for this Friday's porch happy hour. For once the stars had aligned and everyone was in town and available. That was cause for celebration with special food and wine.

Plus, it was February. The cold weather still had us in its grip, but the days were longer and the nights shorter. Spring was a little more than a month away.

And Valentine's Day was next week.

Eli had proposed to me on a Valentine's Day. Every year he would bring me flowers, cook me dinner, and give me a hand-made card, telling me it had been the best day of his life when I'd said yes. Throughout our married life, Valentine's Day had been just as important as the anniversary of our wedding day.

Even after the accident, he'd painstakingly drawn and hand-lettered Valentine's Day cards for me each year. I still had every one of those cards upstairs in a keepsake box.

This will be the first year I won't get a card from him. I blinked back tears at the thought. It would be a tough day for me, but I'd get through it, just like I'd gotten through so many other anniversaries this past year. I'd remember. I'd celebrate what we'd shared. Then I'd keep moving forward.

Maybe I'd be the one who made a card for Eli this year. As I took the charcuterie platters out of the fridge, I thought more about how I should honor the day. I'd make a card. I'd take flowers and the card to the cemetery, and Eli and I would have one last Valentine's Day together. Times like this I missed the presence of his ghost. I knew it was wrong to want him to stay with me after his death. It wasn't fair to tie his spirit to this plane of existence. And it wasn't fair to myself to live my life in the past when I hopefully had several decades' worth of life ahead of me.

Honor the past. Look toward the future.

Today was about the future. I balanced the charcuterie platters and headed to the porch, thrilled to see that Daisy had already arrived. My best friend was pouring herself a big glass of Chardonnay with gloved hands, the scarf I'd knitted and given her for Christmas peeking out from the neckline of her puffy winter coat.

"I brought some fresh bread from the bakery and a few of their fruit spreads." She pulled off one glove to snag a piece of cheese from the platter I was carrying and pop it into her mouth. "Kat is bringing a Crockpot with meatballs, and Olive said she and Suzette are bringing cookies. By the way, did you hear Olive's news?"

"No, what's up with Olive?" I set the trays down and went to pour a glass of wine for myself.

"She. Got. A. Puppy," Daisy announced with a squeal of glee.

I laughed because she sounded exactly like Madison at that moment.

"She's bringing it tonight." Daisy looked around the porch. "I wonder how Taco is going to take the canine addition to our happy hour?"

Oh my. That might be a problem. Taco liked to tease the neighborhood dogs while safely on the other side of the fence. I didn't have much faith that tonight's introduction would go well. A puppy would be loud and exuberant, and Taco did not do well with loud and exuberant, especially when it was inside his personal domain.

"Is it a small puppy?" Hopefully Olive would have it on a leash, or in one of those tiny-dog purses.

"It's a French Bulldog." Daisy scowled into her wine. "I

hate to be *that* person. Olive is so nice, and I know she's shown dogs in the past. Still, it bothers me."

I turned to my friend in surprise. "You don't like French Bulldogs?"

I'd never met one up close and personal, but they looked adorable with their smushed faces and pointy ears. They seemed to be fun, lively dogs, too—perfect for Olive's personality, in my opinion.

"No, it's not that." Daisy took a quick sip of her wine. "I know Olive would have carefully researched breeders, and that she bought from someone reputable, someone who guarantees genetic health and will always take a dog back no questions asked, but…"

"But you wish she'd gotten a dog from the shelter instead." I knew Daisy so well. She'd dedicated her life to working with troubled teens and had a soft spot for those she felt were unwanted and unloved.

Daisy nodded. "I mean, I get it. If you want to show a dog, or want specific traits and characteristics, or a guarantee of health, then it makes sense to go to a breeder. But I see these animals at the county shelter and at rescues, and my heart aches for them. They might be old, or ugly, or have health challenges, but they deserve love too."

I thought of Taco, the supposedly aloof cat I'd gotten from the shelter the day of Eli's funeral. I couldn't bear to come home to an empty house. I'd been feeling lost, lonely, and had been aching with grief. And there had been a gray tabby who'd needed a home.

It had been the best decision I'd made in the last year—well, that and deciding to open my house up to a roommate or three.

"I think everyone needs to take their own circumstances and needs into consideration when bringing a pet into the family," I thought out loud. "The Larses' dog is from a rescue.

And the Petersons a block over always adopt senior and hospice dogs. That's got to be hard. They only had their last dog for six months before it passed. And like you said, Olive showed dogs years ago. If that's what she wants to do, she can't exactly do it with a mixed breed from the shelter."

Daisy waved a hand, then glanced toward the street where several cars were approaching. "I know, I know. I'm just being a judgmental snob. She has the right to buy whatever dog she wants—one that suits her lifestyle and hobbies. It's not my business. If I'm in tears over rescue and shelter dogs, then I should put my money where my mouth is and go adopt one myself."

"Do you have the time for a dog?" I asked her. "With your work, your volunteer stuff, and J.T.? Maybe you should consider a cat. Taco is wonderful company, and I don't need to take him for walks twice a day."

Daisy took a thoughtful sip of her wine. "I don't know. I like both dogs and cats, but now that I think about it, a dog would be awesome. It would be nice to come home and have someone so overjoyed to see me that they might pee a little."

I laughed. "Well, that's me—or any woman over fifty, it seems. You don't need a pet, you need a female roommate of a certain age. Seriously though, Taco greets me at the door when I come home. He doesn't pee in excitement, but he does act like I'm terribly late and he's been waiting for me for days."

She snorted. "That's because he wants out and to get fed. I'm sure your cat adores you, Kay, but it is a bit different being loved by a dog."

I spied Kat walking out of her house to head over, Crockpot in her arms. The two cars had parked. Suzette and Olive got out of one, and Violet Smith got out of the other. I waved to the girl, glad that she'd accepted my invitation to join us.

Loud yapping rent the air and drew everyone's attention. A small fawn-and-black bundle jumped out of Olive's car and raced toward the walkway, only to come up short at the end of a long leash. Taco strolled up next to me from around the side of the porch and sat, eyeing the stranger, who was bouncing up and down as he barked.

"Cats don't do that," I reminded Daisy.

"So I won't get a puppy. I'll get a nice, well-behaved, adult dog." She glanced down at my cat, who was licking a paw and swiping it over her head. "Or maybe a cat. I should probably keep my options open at this point."

I hid a smirk and went down to greet my guests. Judge Beck had finally returned after taking forever to put the broken chair away. He rounded the porch and made a beeline for us.

"Who is this handsome young man?" The judge reached down and scooped the puppy up.

"This is Fairwood's Dreamy Day at the Beach, known as Gus by his family and friends." Olive beamed like a proud mother discussing her son's exemplary school grades.

Judge Beck held the squirming puppy up and it promptly licked his nose. "Hi there Gus. So by the fancy name I take it he's a show dog?"

"Yep," Suzette chimed in. "Olive missed showing, and I was interested as well. Frenchie's don't have a lot of coat maintenance, and we both liked their personality."

"Plus, Frenchies are popular enough that we don't need to travel quite so far for shows." Olive grimaced. "It's hard to finish a dog when the shows in three surrounding states only have two or three competitors in your breed."

The judge went to put the dog down, then suddenly changed his mind and handed him over to me. "Congratulations on the addition to your family. Let me get you ladies some wine while Taco decides if he's going to allow Gus onto the porch or not."

Taco had moved to the top step of the porch and was staring at us, tail twitching and murder in his eyes. I had a feeling Olive and Suzette might be having their happy hour on the lawn instead of the porch.

"Oh my gosh! Is this the new puppy?" Kat gushed as she joined us, handing the Crockpot off to Judge Beck.

I took the opportunity to unload Gus into her eager arms. Leaving Olive and Suzette to make the appropriate introductions, I followed the judge back to the porch and to Taco.

"Now you listen here." I lowered myself down to sit on the step next to my cat. "Gus is a guest. You don't have to like him, but please don't jeopardize his modeling future by clawing him up. Either stay on the porch and be polite, or you can hang out in the shrubberies. Or in the house."

The cat ignored me, gaze fixed on the four-legged intruder, tail still twitching.

"I mean it Taco." I waved a finger at him. "Be nice, or take yourself elsewhere."

"Should I put him inside?" Judge Beck stopped beside me, two glasses of wine balanced in one hand. He extended my glass with the other.

I took the wine, stood, and dusted my pants off. "No, he can escape the porch if he needs to. Gus is leashed, and I'm sure Olive will put him back in the car if he gets too rowdy."

The judge's gaze drifted across the lawn to where Olive, Suzette, Kat and Violet stood with an ecstatic Gus rolling on the brown winter grass. "He's a cute little guy, isn't he? Growing up, I always wanted an English Bulldog, but now I'm thinking my dream dog might be one of those."

"Oh, not you too." I laughed. "Daisy is already talking about getting a dog from the shelter. Am I going to come home one day to find Gus's brother or sister chasing Taco around the house?"

He stiffened. "I'd never do something like that without your agreement." His hands clenched, then his shoulders dropped. "Sorry. I didn't mean to snap at you. Heather's allergic to cats, and I always wanted us to get a dog—especially once the kids had gotten older. She refused every time I brought it up. Said she'd be the one stuck taking care of it and that she had enough to do."

"I'm sorry." I wasn't sure what I was apologizing for. I hadn't done anything wrong. I guess it was because I hated that he and Heather had fought over this.

But partners fought. You couldn't share a life with all its messy responsibilities without occasionally arguing. Eli and I had gone through some doozies in our marriage. There were a few times we could have gone either way. Somehow we'd always made it through the storm.

The ladies and the excited puppy headed toward the porch. Another car came down the street, parking a few houses away where there still was space on the curb. I recognized it as Matt Poffenburger's. I was so glad he'd been able to make it tonight. I hadn't seen him since mid-November, when I'd met him at the nursing home to have lunch with his father. I'd truly enjoyed helping him with various fundraisers and charity events this past year and hoped that his coming here tonight meant we could continue that friendship.

I waved at him, and he jogged through the grass to join the crowd.

"Wine, ladies?" Judge Beck offered the glasses to Olive and Suzette as they climbed the steps. "Kat? Violet? What would you like? I'm serving today."

Violet blushed red, her eyes fixed on the steps. "Just a soda, please. I need to drive home after this and I'm a total lightweight."

I had to smile at her sudden shyness. Judge Beck could be an imposing figure, and even though she'd been attending the occasional happy hour for over a month, Violet still seemed to be flustered around him.

"Well, *I'm* walking across the street and down one house," Kat announced. "So bring on the wine!"

"I'll help pour," Matt said. "but I'd rather have a beer if you've got any."

"In the kitchen," the judge told him. "Let's get these ladies situated, then we'll go raid the fridge."

The two men headed off to the table while Violet paused on the steps and knelt down to stroke Taco.

"That puppy is cute, but you're still the king of the porch," she told the purring cat.

I snorted. "He's the king of everything he surveys."

"I've actually been thinking of getting a cat myself," Violet confided. "Now that I've got a good job and a place of my own, it would be nice to have a furry companion."

"The shelters will be full of kittens soon," Kat told her. "You'll have a lot to choose from."

"I think I might get an adult cat instead." Violet picked Taco up. The cat snuggled against her, kneading her arm with soft paws, the perfect ambassador for the adoption of adult cats.

"I'm thinking of adding a pet to my household as well," Daisy said. "A dog. Or a cat. I'm not sure yet."

"Trust me, dogs are more work." Kat laughed. "I love Atlas, but he's glued to my side when I'm home. I can't even go to the bathroom without him whining and scratching at the door. The guests love him, though."

"Taco sometimes does the same thing when I'm in the bathroom," I told her. "There I am, having a private moment, and suddenly there's meowing and a little furry paw reaching under the door."

Daisy chuckled. "Guess I'll need to learn to pee with the door closed."

"That or have a dog sitting smack in front of you, staring as you go," Kat told her.

"Or a cat trying to climb onto your lap when you're on the toilet," I added.

"So, are you heading to the shelter this weekend to see what's available?" Judge Beck asked Daisy as he and Matt handed out glasses of wine and Violet's soda.

"I think so." Daisy pursed her lips. "The Milford County Shelter first, then maybe I'll hit up the Oxbridge County one as well."

"Don't forget the rescues," Violet said. "Especially if there's a particular breed you're looking for."

"Ooo, you have to check out Second Chance Rescue," Kat chimed in. "Prucilla Downing is a saint."

"Wasn't she involved in shutting down that puppy mill last month?" Olive asked. "It was all over the papers."

"Yes, but I think most of that was because of Free the Fur." Violet made a face. "That group is a little extreme, but I've never heard anything but good about Prucilla Downing and her rescue."

"Puppy mill?" Had this happened when we'd been skiing? This was the first I'd heard of it.

"Just outside of Milford near Washdale," Kat said. "The guy was breeding purebred dogs two litters a year from their first heat until they could no longer have pups, then he'd dump them at a rescue or a shelter. He was selling the puppies to pet shops all over the country. No one knew about it until Free the Fur and Prucilla Downing got involved. Like Violet said, Free the Fur can be extreme and controversial, but they were the ones who fought to have the puppy mill investigated. Second Chance Rescue coordinated the foster care for the animals after the seizure, though. Prucilla made sure the dogs got immediate veterinary care and had places to go with people who understood the challenges of caring for neglected and unsocialized dogs."

"Wow." I'd clearly missed that huge local story.

"I read about that," Daisy chimed in. "I hadn't realized Prucilla Downing ran a dog rescue though, I just thought she was active in animal welfare."

"She does both," Violet told her. "Her rescue scored really high on NonProfitRating.com. The woman is dedicated."

"She is," Kat said. "Second Chance Rescue has transported dogs from kill shelters out of state to be fostered and adopted. They also take in injured dogs and cats that some shelters don't have the funds to help. She's a saint."

"She sometimes has puppies available for adoption too," Violet added. "Shelters can't manage the bottle-babies or a litter of underage pups with their mom, so she takes them in."

"How big is her facility?" I wondered. The woman must have a farm and a sizable staff to accommodate all those animals.

"Oh, she's just got a regular sized house and yard. Most of the animals are with one of her foster care people, so she doesn't have them onsite." Violet set Taco down. "She has a website where you can see all of the adoptable animals. Then you fill out an application. They interview you, do a visit to your home, and if everything looks okay, they arrange for you to meet the pet at their foster home."

Daisy laughed. "Wow, that's like adopting a child!"

"She wants to make sure the animals go to a great home," Kat replied. "After all those poor dogs and cats have been through in their lives, I don't blame her at all."

Daisy lifted her hands. "Oh, I understand, really. I just don't want to go through all that only to find out at the meet-

and-greet that the dog and I aren't a good match. I'd rather meet the dog first, *then* jump through all the hoops."

Kat laughed. "Well, definitely check out the shelter, then. But you should still go to Second Chance Rescue. She does have some adoptable pets onsite, and she might make an exception and let you meet a dog first if you're interested in one that's in foster."

Daisy nodded. "I'll do that. Are you free tomorrow, Kay? Shall we spend the day visiting shelters and rescues? Lunch is on me."

I hesitated. I was such a sucker for animals in need. I'd walked into a shelter the day of my husband's funeral and left with a cat. There was a reasonable chance I might come home tomorrow with another cat. Or a dog. Or both.

"I'll go, but you can't let me adopt any animal without waiting at least a week," I told Daisy.

There. That should give me plenty of opportunity to be objective about my ability to care for another animal. *And* let Judge Beck weigh in. I was sure the kids would give an enthusiastic thumbs-up to any additional four-legged resident, but it would be the judge and I who would need to provide the care. And there was Taco to think of. He was definitely the king of the house, and I didn't want to bring any newcomer in who would upset him and make him unhappy.

My attention was diverted by the yap-yap of Gus as he happily sniffed my porch. Olive kept him close, letting Gus explore but not giving him enough leash to jump up on people's legs or knock any of the porch furniture over. Gus suddenly noticed Taco over by the table with the food and strained at the end of the leash.

"Uh oh." Olive handed her wine glass to Suzette and scooped the pup into her arms.

"If you know what's good for you, you'll be respectful to

that cat," she told the puppy before turning to face the feline. "Taco, my man, are you going to accept Gus into your domain?"

Taco stuck his tail in the air, but didn't seem particularly bothered by Gus's presence. Olive slowly set the pup down once more, shortening the leash.

Gus sniffed the floor, finding something more interesting than the cat. Pausing, he began licking at something on the porch decking that I couldn't see. Taco watched him for a few seconds, then wandered close to sniff whatever Gus was licking. The pair stood there, nose to nose, and I breathed a sigh of relief.

Then Gus looked up, apparently startled to see Taco in front of him. With a quick step backward, he let out a sharp bark.

Taco ignored him, still sniffing at the spot Gus had been licking.

The dog barked once more. I tensed when Taco looked up at the pup and swiped his face with a paw, but the cat kept his claws retracted and the move seemed more playful than any sort of warning.

Gus sat down on his butt and tilted his head as he regarded the cat. He didn't bark. Taco swatted him again with a soft paw, then returned to sniffing the porch while the puppy stared at him.

So far so good. I decided that Taco must have been exposed to dogs before and wasn't particularly bothered by them. And Gus seemed smart enough to know where he stood in relation to the feline of the house. After watching Taco for a few seconds, Gus laid down and let out a big sigh.

Well. That obviously was one less thing I needed to worry about.

"Tell us all about your new puppy," Violet said to Olive. "Where did you get him? How did you decide on this particular breed? Are you really going to show him, or is he just a pet?"

Olive beamed. "I've *always* loved French Bulldogs. When I was little, I showed our family dog in 4H, then started taking my Boston Terrier to AKC shows after college. I always wanted a French Bulldog, though."

"I had no idea you showed dogs," Kat commented.

Olive shrugged. "It was a fun hobby. My Boston Terrier wasn't bringing home any trophies, and I wasn't planning on breeding her, but I loved the competition and comradery of the dogs shows. I decided I wanted to get back into that sort of thing."

"Well, Gus is definitely adorable," I chimed in. "I don't know much about breed standards, but I'd give him a trophy if I were a judge."

"Oh, he's got an impressive pedigree," Suzette told me. "Once we found out Gus was sired by Wilmont's Heart of a Lion, we knew he was the puppy for us."

Olive dug a paper out of her purse and unfolded it before passing it around. "Here's a copy of Gus's lineage. Denny Topper at Fairwoods Kennel has exclusive rights to breed Grand Champion Wilmont's Heart of a Lion. Lion was twice Best of Breed at Westminster. He came close to winning Best in Show one year. He was the absolute standard as far as French Bulldogs were twenty years ago. I've got a list from the AKC of all the registered puppies Lion has sired over the last ten years, and it's only a hundred and twenty. We were lucky to get Gus."

I did the math. "Wait. How old is this Heart of a Lion dog if he was winning dog shows twenty years ago? And how is he still having puppies?"

Daisy laughed. "Doggie Viagra? Please tell me it's doggie Viagra!"

Olive chuckled. "No, it's not doggie Viagra. Wilmont's

Heart of a Lion died fifteen years ago. Denny Topper at Fairwoods Kennel is another French Bulldog breeder. He bought the stock and breeding rights from Gus Wilmont's estate after he died. Smartest thing he ever did."

"Breeding rights to a long dead dog? How exactly does that work?" Daisy asked. I was glad that I wasn't the only one confused about this whole thing.

"Straws." Suzette held up both hands and shrugged. "It's sounds like science-fiction, but evidently it's been a thing since the nineteen-sixties. Cryopreservation. Frozen semen. If you've got a dog with some amazing genes, you can freeze his stuff and he'll be siring puppies long after he's gone."

My mouth dropped open. "Even fifteen years later? Doesn't it degrade or something?"

"Nope. It's good indefinitely," Olive said. "They use liquid nitrogen. When they thaw it out, they rate the motility and that determines how many straws you need, but the swimmers are still good."

Wow. I hadn't known any of this at all. And I couldn't believe we were standing on my front porch at Friday happy hour, discussing frozen dog semen.

Olive went on to talk about her pup's genetic background and how she'd decided to call him Gus to honor Gus Wilmont, the breeder of the puppy's sire over two decades ago. Looking over, I saw that the pup and Taco were busy ignoring each other. The cat had jumped up into a porch chair and was curled up on the cushion with Gus sniffing away underneath. Taco didn't seem bothered at all by our canine guest, and Gus was clearly more interested in what food people may have dropped on the ground than the cat.

Judge Beck moved to stand beside me, while Matt, with a beer in his hand, joined the conversation about Gus's impressive lineage.

"They seem to be getting along okay." The judge nodded toward Taco and the puppy.

"Thankfully yes." I smiled up at him. "It's a relief. We'll be able to get our puppy fix on Friday evenings when Olive brings this little guy over. All the joy, and none of the work."

"And a happy cat. Or at least a cat who doesn't seem particularly disturbed to be sharing the porch with a puppy."

"Did you mean it when you said you might be interested in a dog?" I asked him. "Daisy plans to drag me around to half a dozen rescues and shelters tomorrow. Obviously I wouldn't make any split-second decisions, but if you really want a dog, I can keep my eyes open."

"It's your decision whether or not we get a dog. Honestly, I'm happy with just Taco."

"I think I'm happy with just Taco, too." I remembered what he'd said about Heather and decided I needed to elaborate. "It's not just *my* decision, you know. You live here too. I would never adopt a dog or another cat without getting your input first. And I'd absolutely respect your decision on whether you wanted a new four-legged roommate or not. I just want you to know that I'm open to discussion and compromise on these kinds of things. If you really want a dog, now or in the future, I'll be open to discussing the idea. Although I kind of like just having Taco right now, your opinion and your wants are important too."

He smiled. "I appreciate that. I don't really think it's a good time to add another pet to the household. I'll admit I was a little worried about your intent when you started asking questions about Gus's parentage and the breeders, though."

"Come on, you didn't find all that fascinating?" I elbowed him and grinned. "Frozen semen from a long dead dog. It's almost like a science fiction novel."

"Or a horror novel," he teased. "A zombie dog, passing on strange genetic traits through cytogenetic breeding."

I looked over at the puppy. "If Gus's head spins around or his eyes glow, I'm running for the house and locking the door behind me."

"I'll grab the wine on my way in." Judge Beck shifted to look at Gus as well. "Think he'll start eating brains? Mind-controlling Olive and Suzette? Levitating objects with a wave of his paw?"

"I hope not. Good thing he's all of seven pounds right now. I think we can fight him off," I said.

The judge shook his head. "I've read the books and watched the television shows. Seven pounds of zombie dog is still seven pounds of zombie dog. I'd rather grab the wine and run than try to fight an undead puppy."

"Taco would defend us," I told him, knowing Taco would probably be the first one in the door. Or maybe not. The cat had proven to be a good defense against poltergeists—especially when the ghosts messed with his food.

"His parentage might have horror-movie potential, but I think we're safe. At least for tonight." Judge Beck reached out a hand for my empty wineglass. "Can I get you a refill?"

I looked around at all my friends here on my front porch, laughing and enjoying themselves. The heater gave off just enough warmth to keep us comfortable. There was food and drink and companionship. And a puppy now, in addition to my cat. I loved this tradition I'd started just after Judge Beck moved in. I loved the direction my life had taken after tragedy had left me wondering what the future held.

My heart felt close to bursting with sudden happiness. And as for another wine...well, just like Kat, I didn't have far to walk.

I slid the empty wineglass into the judge's gloved hand. "Thank you. I *would* like a refill."

CHAPTER 2

*D*aisy arrived promptly at seven the next morning, because a day of puppy shopping was no excuse to miss our morning yoga.

We'd been doing our practice in the basement if the temperature dipped too low, but this morning it was sunny with temps right around freezing, so we braved the outdoors. Our breath still steamed in the chill air, but it felt bright and cheerful, and it wasn't so cold that my gloved hands were going numb. The sun sent its thin rays through the slats in my fencing, striping the brown grass as well as our yoga mats. We breathed in and out to a count of eight, did a few warm-up movements, then got down to business. Daisy had a set of vinyasas that she always liked to start the day with. After a few rounds of planks, cobra poses, and warrior poses in her modified Sun Salutation routine, we moved into meat of our practice. Some days that included endless boat poses to work our core, or pigeon poses to open up our hips.

Today's practice was different.

Balance was not my friend. I used to joke that I probably

couldn't pass a field sobriety test stone sober. Walk in a straight line? Not going to happen. Stand on one foot? Impossible. Stand on one foot, then hinge forward at the hip while extending the other leg straight out? Not in a million years. But that's what Daisy was doing. I did my best to follow, trying not to fall on my face.

Focusing my vision fixed on a bare tree as a means to keep my balance, I slowly lifted my leg. Then quickly set it down again. I needed something to hold on to—a stick or a wall. But neither option was available, so I kept picking up my foot and putting it down, holding the pose for only a few seconds at a time. Finally Daisy lowered her leg, moving on to the next pose.

Copying her, I skated my arms across my chest, then bent my elbows to tangle them like vines twisting together. Eagle arms Daisy had called this, although nothing about the pose looked or felt like an eagle to me.

"Raise your left knee," she instructed.

I slowly lifted my leg, wobbling a bit as I tried to maintain my balance.

"Now cross your left foot over your right knee and hook that foot behind your calf, twisting your legs like your arms."

"You've got to be kidding," I complained. "That's impossible."

"Fix your gaze on something still, something on the horizon, and breathe. Then cross your left foot over the right knee, and hook it behind your calf," she repeated.

I did as she said, hoping I could get my legs untwisted fast enough to catch my balance if I fell.

Daisy's morning yoga practice usually featured lots of planks with transitions to things like downward dog, cobra, or warriors one and two. Where the heck had she come up with this twisty stuff? I risked sending my friend a quick glare and nearly toppled over.

"Breathe into the twist," she said.

"Can't breathe when I'm a pretzel," I grumbled. I did as she said and held the pose for all of five seconds before having to untwist and put my other foot down. Five seconds. I got the feeling that would be a record for me.

Thankfully, the rest of our morning's practice involved keeping both feet on the ground. Balance. As much as I'd hated the twisting, one-legged stuff, maybe this was something I needed to work on. When Daisy and I had first started our morning yoga, I'd been about as flexible as a brick. Simple poses felt clunky and awkward. Moving from downward dog into a forward fold had required some embarrassing hopping instead of the fluid, smooth movement I was capable of now. Throughout the years, my strength and flexibility had improved. I was confident my balance would as well if we continued practicing these types of poses.

Practice. Patience. Persistence. Acceptance and surrender about what was, but still keeping the faith that I could always improve, always progress and move forward. That wasn't just about yoga, it was about life.

After we'd finished, we went inside for a quick cup of coffee. Daisy headed home to shower and change in preparation for our outing and I went upstairs to do the same, coming down to find Judge Beck in the kitchen, pouring himself a mug of coffee. Warmth rolled through me as I took him in. Mussed hair. Quirky flamingo-print pajama bottoms that one of the kids had given him. A threadbare, pub T-shirt. Bare feet. He sent me a lopsided smile, and my heart galloped into overdrive.

"I thought you'd be off with Daisy already, scouring the shelters and rescues for a potential addition to her household."

"As soon as she gets back," I told him. "This morning's yoga took a little longer than usual."

He replaced the coffee pot and leaned back against the counter, taking a sip from his mug. "What time do you think you'll be home? Should I make dinner for us? Pick up take out?"

The thought of the judge cooking for me, of a hot meal and a good-looking man waiting for me when I got home, made me smile. "Oh, I'd love that! Either one. There's a chicken in the fridge or some porkchops in the freezer you can thaw out if you want. But I'm up for anything—whether you're cooking or picking something up."

"Is six o'clock okay?"

I nodded. "It shouldn't take us too long to visit two shelters and three rescues, but you know Daisy."

He laughed. "Yes, I do."

I walked over to refill my coffee cup and stood next to him in silence. The silence grew long and awkward. The judge fidgeted and finally turned to me, setting his coffee cup on the counter.

"I...uh...I wanted to ask what you've got planned for Valentines' Day. I mean, I don't want to presume anything. It's just that *I'm* obviously not doing anything. And I thought that if you weren't, we could maybe go out to dinner or something?"

Oh. *Oh.* I was so pleased he'd said something, that he actually wanted to take me out to dinner on a night that was set aside for romance. Ever since we'd come back from the ski trip, things had been different between us. We stood closer together. We touched—a hand on a shoulder, or a quick brush of our fingers as we passed a plate over dinner. There was an expectation that we ate together, that we shared our schedule for the day and made time to do things together. To others it might seem like our relationship was moving painfully slow, but I loved it. I enjoyed exploring the potential of "us" without the rushed, frenzied pace of my youth. I enjoyed the tingly tension that stretched tighter between us with each touch.

Valentine's Day dinner. It would be one more step forward for us, and I was excited to take that step.

But Eli. I'd meant for this Valentines' Day to be a sort of goodbye for Eli and me, a last reconnect on a holiday that we'd always considered to be ours. It felt disloyal to change my memorial plans to go out with a man who I was slowly falling for. Yes, I needed to move on, but it hadn't even been a full year yet since Eli died, and with that anniversary coming up, I was struggling. Why couldn't Judge Beck have come into my life after a few years, when I was done mourning my husband?

But I'd probably never truly stop mourning Eli. And Judge Beck had come along at the perfect time. I would have lost more than my home without him. He and the kids had made this year something wonderful when it could have been full of desperation and bleak sorrow. No one was guaranteed tomorrow, and I'd be a fool to let this chance at happiness pass me by.

"I'd love to have Valentine's Day dinner with you, but there's something I really need to do beforehand. Can we make late reservations? Like around seven?"

I figured that I'd go to the cemetery first, have my last Valentines' Day with Eli, then go out with the Judge. But even that felt wrong, like I was dating two different guys on the same night in secret. No, I needed to handle this differently.

If the judge was truly going to be a part of my life, then I needed to open all of myself to him. If he wasn't okay with my grief for Eli, with the things I needed to do to remember my husband and honor our marriage, then this relationship wouldn't work out anyway.

"Sure. Seven is fine. I'll make the reservations and organize everything."

Now it was me shifting my feet and feeling awkward as I tried to find the right words to say. "Um, that thing I have to do?" I met his eyes and took a breath. "I wanted to go to Eli's grave site. I wanted to make him a card and bring him flowers, like he always did for me. He proposed on Valentine's Day, and it's always been our special time."

The judge looked horrified. "Kay, I'm so sorry. I didn't know. It was completely insensitive for me to invite you out to dinner on a day that meant so much to you both. We can do it another night."

"No." I put a hand on his chest, feeling his heartbeat through the threadbare T-shirt. "I want to spend Valentine's Day with you. I'm excited for us to go out for a romantic dinner together. It's just that there are things I need to do—that I will always need to do—to honor and remember what I had with Eli. I want...I want a future and I hope that my future includes you. But I can't erase my past."

He reached up and put his hand over mine, holding my fingers in place. "I don't want you to erase your past. If it feels too weird for us to go out on a day that was a special anniversary between you and Eli, then I understand. Don't feel like you have to rush your remembrance plans to have dinner with me. We can go out another night, if you want. There's no reason we can't celebrate our Valentine's Day on the fifteenth, or even the following week."

But that wasn't what I wanted to do. I didn't want my past and my future to have some hard barrier between them.

"Make reservations for seven," I told him. "If it's okay with you, I'd like us to go out to the cemetery together before we head to dinner. I'll take a few moments to remember the life that Eli and I shared, to place the flowers and card at the gravesite. Then we'll go have a lovely, romantic dinner together."

Did that sound weird? Was it odd that I wanted to combine mourning my husband's loss with the celebration of a new love? For me, it didn't feel strange.

"Are you sure you want me there?" The judge's eyes searched my face. "Do you want me to come to the gravesite with you? Or wait in the SUV?"

"That's entirely up to you," I told him.

He let out a long breath. "I don't know. Do you think he'd approve? Of us? I don't want to be disrespectful."

I stepped closer to him. "Eli would have liked you. And I think you would have liked him, too. He wanted me to be happy. I know he'd approve."

The judge took my hand in his and lifted it to his cheek, briefly holding it there before turning his head and kissing my palm.

"I'm glad. And I'm glad we have a date. Now, you go have fun with Daisy and make sure she doesn't adopt half a dozen rescue dogs. I'll have dinner ready when you get home."

There was a knock on the door, then a cheerful "hello" as Daisy walked in. I slid my hand free, still feeling the touch of the judge's lips against my palm. Everything seemed to be coming together. Everything felt so right. As much as I was looking forward to dog-shopping with Daisy, I was more excited about dinner tonight with the judge—*and* our Valentine's Day date.

"One dog," I assured Judge Beck as I grabbed my purse off the kitchen island. "I'm going to make sure Daisy only brings home one dog. I promise."

CHAPTER 3

$\mathcal{O}$ur first stop was Second Chance Rescue. Daisy had checked out the available dogs via the rescue website and made an appointment to discuss a few she was potentially interested in. We pulled up to the neat, two-story house, deep within a large housing development just outside of Milford. Even with the cold lingering in the February air, people were out jogging, walking their dogs, and sweeping off walkways.

Prucilla Downing answered the door at our first knock. The woman looked to be about my age. Strands of silver hair had escaped her messy bun and floated around her face. Her kind blue eyes had deep crinkles at the corners. Pet hair clung to her jeans and her sweatshirt, and she dusted her hands off on a rag before reaching out to shake Daisy's and my hands.

"Daisy! And you must be Kay. Come in, come in. Excuse the mess. I've got a litter of puppies in from out of state that have been quarantining in the dining room and they are rambunctious little escape artists."

We entered and followed her past the dining room where

a mess of puppies raced and jumped around an area cordoned off into a pen by what looked to be a series of interconnected baby gates. Prucilla led us to a kitchen and gestured for us to sit.

"I pulled pictures of the two dogs you wanted to consider, as well as another that I think might interest you."

She slid three glossy eight-by-tens in front of Daisy. I scooted closer to my friend to look. One dog looked like he had a lot of border collie in his parentage, the other two were truly of the Heinz 57 variety—one with short, tan fur and a smushed snout, the other was brindle with floppy ears on a broad head.

Prucilla pointed to the collie. "Zippy is four or five years old and came from a shelter in Ohio. Zip needs to be in a home with no young children since he can be a bit exuberant. He loves playing fetch, going for long walks, and car rides to the park."

"Does he like piña coladas?" I teased. "And getting caught in the rain?"

"He has to be into yoga," Daisy reminded me. "I can take or leave the health food thing, but yoga is a must."

Prucilla ignored us. I got the feeling as cheerful and pleasant as she was, when it came to her dogs, she didn't joke around.

"Zip was heartworm positive when we got him, but he's gone through his treatment and is fully recovered. He's healthy and ready for his forever home with someone active who has a fenced-in yard."

"Sounds promising," Daisy told her. "What about this guy? The one that looks like a Labrador and a Pug got it on? I saw him on the website and thought he was cute."

"That's Snickers. He came to us two months ago as an owner surrender. His people lost their house to foreclosure and they couldn't find a rental property that would allow a dog over twenty-five pounds. Snickers is eight years old, has some allergies that require a daily pill, and he needs special shampoo, but other than that he's in perfect health. He's good with children and cats, and his favorite thing is to snuggle up on the couch next to you."

Daisy elbowed me. "Good with cats."

"That doesn't mean Taco will be good with him, though," I warned her.

It *would* be nice if Daisy could bring her dog over while we did our morning yoga. Her new buddy could come in the house afterward and have a Milk-Bone as we drank our coffee. Taco had seemed to accept Olive's rowdy puppy, so surely he'd be okay with this sedate dog?

I looked at the pictures once more, thinking Zip might be too...well, zippy, and that Snickers might be too sedate. Maybe this third dog would be the perfect in-between, like the baby bear's just-right porridge.

"This one is Max." Prucilla pointed to the brindle, floppy-eared dog. "He's six years old and lived on a farm until his owner died. Max is good with kids and all other animals. He's taken to indoor living well, but still loves to spend lots of time outside. He can have a little anxiety when he's left alone, so you'd need to crate him when you're gone. That said, I really don't want him to go to a home where he's in a crate eight hours a day. Ideally I'd like to see him in a situation with a stay-at-home parent, or a retired person. But you said you could possibly take any dog you adopt to work with you?"

Daisy nodded. "Yes, but there *would* be times he might need to stay in an office by himself, though."

Prucilla pursed her lips, picking up the picture of Max for a few seconds before putting it back down again. "That might work, but you'd need to be patient with him. He'd probably be anxious at first when you leave, and he might bark a bit before he settles down."

Patience wouldn't be a problem for Daisy. She worked with troubled teens. If she could be patient with them, then Max would be easy, but the barking? I wasn't sure how her co-workers would feel about that. I glanced at the three pictures, thinking that none of them felt just-right. Maybe the shelters or one of the other rescues would have that perfect dog for Daisy to adopt.

A forlorn howl came from somewhere in the house. Prucilla grimaced.

"Sorry. That's our newest arrival, Lady. I better go check on her."

She got up and Daisy and I both rose to go with her to see this new dog. We followed Prucilla to the living room, where a crate stood with a blanket draped over the top. Inside was a thin dog with matted, wiry hair. Lady pawed anxiously at the cage door as one of the puppies from the other room bounced in front of the confined dog. The puppy dropped into a play-bow, its tail wagging, and Lady howled once more.

"Oh, these puppies will be the death of me," Prucilla exclaimed as she bent to scoop up the escapee. "Let me return him to the other room. I'll be right back."

This time we didn't follow her. Daisy approached the cage and squatted down, putting herself at eye-level with the dog inside.

"Hey Lady. You look like you could use a good meal or five, poor thing."

I expected Lady to cringe away from Daisy, but her tail wagged furiously and she pressed her bony side against the cage. Her matted fur was dirty, and a scab from some injury made a rusty diagonal line across her muzzle.

"Sorry about that," Prucilla said as she came back to the room. "Those puppies are a handful."

"Aren't they all?" Daisy put her fingers through the cage to scratch Lady's ear. "What's this girl's story?"

Prucilla knelt down beside her. "Lady came to me from a local hoarding situation. I just got her in this morning, and I haven't had time to bathe her yet or shave these mats out of her fur. I'll take her in to get a vet check and shots Monday."

Daisy stood and Lady barked in protest, her tail still wagging happily.

"She likes you," Prucilla commented as she rose to her feet.

"I like her too," Daisy said.

Oh my. I knew my friend well enough to recognize that she more than liked this filthy terrier-mix in the cage. Lady was wiggling her way into Daisy's heart.

"What's she like?" I asked. Zippy had seemed too energetic for Daisy's lifestyle, and Snickers too sedate. And Max had those separation issues. Lady had been quiet here in her crate until the puppy had come in to tease her. She didn't seem overly excited, or too quiet.

Prucilla held up both hands. "It's hard to tell this soon. She seems smart and well socialized. I don't know what health issues she might have, and I haven't had a chance to test her for things like food or toy aggression yet."

"I can work with any of that. I think...I think I'm interested in this one. We've still got other places to visit today, but I'm thinking this might be the dog for me," Daisy said. Lady stared adoringly up at her, clearly feeling the same.

"I really don't like to adopt dogs out until they've spent a few weeks with one of our fosters, so we can tell what their personalities are like," Prucilla replied. "You said you haven't had a dog since you were a child, and I don't want your first rescue to be a bad fit."

"I could wait." Daisy knelt down again to pet Lady. "We could see how she does with her foster family for a few weeks, and I can decide then. I just started looking today. Waiting for a week or two isn't unreasonable."

"Absolutely. And adopting from a rescue isn't like buying from a store," Prucilla warned. "There are applications and interviews and a site visit of your house. Two to three weeks is common. Even if you decide to adopt a dog from the shelter, it still would take a few days to a week to process your application."

"I could always sign up to foster her myself," Daisy mused. "If she's not a good fit, then I've still given her a good foundation to find a home with someone else."

Prucilla wrinkled her nose. "Fostering is hard. It's difficult to take care of an animal for weeks or months, then have to say goodbye when they go to another home. It takes a special kind of person to do that. I don't want to dissuade you, but I want you to know that it's not easy to let go, even if the dog isn't a perfect fit for you. Plus, since you haven't had a dog in so long, I'd worry placing an unknown like Lady with you, to be honest."

"I understand. Can you tell me a bit more about fostering, though? What it involves, and what you expect from someone who is fostering one of your dogs?" Daisy asked.

I wandered around the room as Prucilla went over things like housebreaking, leash-walking, and working with separation anxiety and food aggression. The room's hardwood floors were marked after what looked like years of traffic by four-legged canines with untrimmed nails. The sofa cushions were worn. The end table had a leg that had been used as a chew toy. The French doors looking out to the fenced-in backyard were covered in nose prints.

I loved it. As someone who had cat hair on all her furniture, and who was constantly shooing Taco off the kitchen counters, I appreciated a woman who clearly wasn't worried about the contributions her rescues had made to her home décor.

Making my way over to the fireplace, I eyed the trophies, pictures, and plaques lined up along the mantle with surprise. They were dog-show awards. Best Dog. Best in Breed. Best in Show. Bred, Owned, and Showed. From the pictures on the wall and the script on each of the awards, it looked like Prucilla had once been a breeder of show-quality Boxers. I hadn't pegged Prucilla-the-animal-rescuer for someone who bred dogs, let alone showed them, but I guessed a passion for dogs and animal advocacy didn't have to exclude either.

"I'll definitely be in touch," Daisy said.

I turned around to find Prucilla and my friend shaking hands. With another quick glance at the trophies, I rejoined them. We made our way to the door, and I waited until we had driven out of the subdivision before I spoke.

"Well? Who's at the top of your list right now?" I knew, but I wanted to hear it from Daisy herself.

She sighed. "Lady. And she *shouldn't* be at the top of my list. I don't know anything about her, and neither does Prucilla. I realize some of my interest might be because she's the only dog I've met in person today. The others are just pictures right now, and it's hard to gauge chemistry with a picture. I should be looking at Snickers. He might be a little too chill, but that wouldn't necessarily be a bad thing. Max sounded good, although the separation anxiety would be something I'd need to work with. I think Zippy would be too energetic for me."

"Snickers does seem like he'd be a nice dog," I agreed.

"But Lady..." Daisy shrugged. "I don't know. I just got a feeling when I saw her there. I don't want to make a snap decision though."

"And we do have other dogs to visit," I reminded her. "The Milford County shelter had some cuties on their website."

"Plus the other shelter, and then there's breed specific rescues I can look into." Daisy glanced over at me. "It's sad. So many dogs in need of a home. I wish I could take them all, but one is all I have time for."

"Then make sure it's the perfect one. Whether that's Lady, or Snickers, or another dog. You've got plenty of time to decide. Sadly, I don't think these dogs are going to be snatched up in the next few weeks while you consider all of your options and fill out applications."

Daisy nodded. "True. I've got plenty of time. And thanks to rescuers like Prucilla, foster families, and the employees and volunteers at our county shelter, these dogs have plenty of time as well."

I shuddered, thinking of other shelters where overcrowding meant some animals never got a chance to find a forever home. I hated that healthy, loving animals were put to sleep due to a lack of room or funding. Maybe I should be looking at my budget and seeing if there was room in there for monthly donations to a local shelter or rescue. Maybe I should be volunteering. Or fostering. Taco would always be king of my house, but surely there was room for a temporary guest—either of the canine or feline variety?

No. I swore I wouldn't make an emotional decision. I could make a difference by fundraising and volunteering. Taco was going to remain an only child for the time being. Today I'd look my fill, get in lots of petting and snuggling, but that was it. Daisy was the one looking to adopt a dog, and I was just along for support.

$\mathcal{I}$ was exhausted and hungry. We'd stopped for a quick lunch after visiting the two shelters, then had headed out to see two other rescues. By the time we'd finished looking at the prospective candidates at Forever Love Rescue, it was late afternoon. I thought about Judge Beck and the meal that would be waiting for me when I got home, and didn't care whether he'd decided to cook or not. Heck, he could have served me cardboard and I would have eaten it.

I couldn't wait to get home. We'd eat dinner, then the Judge and I would watch movies downstairs while I propped my feet up and relaxed. But before we headed back to Locust Point and home, Daisy and I had one more stop to make.

She'd made her decision, and now she needed to fill out the application and begin the process to adopt Lady as soon as Prucilla felt the dog was ready for her forever home. We'd pulled over to the side of the road after we'd left the last rescue, and Daisy had made the phone call, letting Prucilla know that Lady was the one for her.

There were so many wonderful animals who needed

homes, and any one of the dogs we'd seen today would have made an amazing companion for my friend. But in the end, the scruffy terrier mix had stolen her heart, and she was convinced that Lady was the dog she wanted.

"Are you sure you don't want to sleep on it?" I asked, knowing that once Daisy made up her mind, she wouldn't change it.

"Nope." She shot me a quick grin. "I'm so excited. You don't mind going back to Prucilla's before we head home, do you? I just want to get the ball rolling."

"Not at all," I assured her. While Daisy was filling out paperwork, maybe I'd play with the puppies. I'd been petting dogs all day, but a person never got tired of four-legged affection and some puppy love would be the perfect way to end the afternoon.

We pulled into Prucilla's driveway, got out, and made our way to the front door, where we immediately heard the sound of barking from inside.

"Must be feeding time," Daisy commented. "Sounds like they're all pretty excited in there."

We knocked, and the barking intensified, but no one answered.

"You let her know we were coming, right?" I asked Daisy.

"Yeah. I told her we were going to swing by on our way home and to expect us in half an hour." Daisy knocked again. "She sounded distracted on the phone. Maybe she's dealing with some new arrivals, or another adopter."

"Or those crazy puppies," I added, smiling as I thought about the little fluff balls.

"She probably can't hear us over all that barking." Daisy turned the handle and opened the door a crack. "Hello? Prucilla? It's Daisy and Kay."

We exchanged a questioning glance, then I pushed the door all the way open. "Prucilla? Hello?"

"Maybe she's downstairs getting food together or something," Daisy said. "We should probably wait here. I don't want her to come up and find us wandering around her house."

That would be horribly rude. And illegal. I doubted Prucilla would have us arrested for trespass though, especially since Daisy was adopting one of her dogs.

I hesitated, then stepped in. "She knows we're coming. We'll just stand in the foyer until she comes back up and can hear us." There was no sense in waiting outside and yelling through an open door when Prucilla was expecting us, and it seemed silly to leave and come back just because she couldn't hear us knocking.

A little ball of brown fur darted past me. Then another with brown fur and black ears.

"The puppies!" I ran after them, Daisy intercepting a third escapee near the stairs.

I managed to scoop one up, but the other evaded my hands and raced toward the living room, merrily barking. I chased after him, heading into the room and sliding to a halt. Prucilla lay on the floor in a pool of blood next to the open dog crate. Beside her was a pile of broken trophies from the now empty mantle and a bunch of shredded chunks of fur.

I dropped the pup from my hands and ran to kneel down beside Prucilla, not sure if I should administer aid, or if it was too late for that. Her eyes stared sightlessly at the ceiling. Her chest was still. Ignoring the blood, I reached out to take her pulse and found none. A shadow flitted at the edge of my vision and moved to stand beside the body, confirming my worst fears.

A ghost. Prucilla's ghost, to be exact.

I heard Daisy gasp. "Oh no! What…is she…?"

"Call 911," I told her as I stood. "She's dead."

Daisy fumbled in her purse, pulling out her cell phone. "Are you sure? Maybe we should do CPR or something."

I glanced at the shadowy figure hovering over the body. "I think it's too late for CPR."

Daisy frantically relayed the situation to the 911 operator. I stood, trying to figure out what had happened. There was nothing Prucilla could have fallen and hit her head on. And even if there were, that wouldn't explain the broken trophies and plaques, or the chunks of fur all over the place.

Conflicted between the knowledge that I shouldn't be tampering with a crime scene, and curiosity over the bits of fur, curiosity won. I picked up a piece, turning it over in my hands. What I'd worried might be some grisly remains of a butchered animal were just fragments of preserved fur. They seemed to be real, since the backing wasn't the woven fabric of fake fur but a hide-like substance. Picking up another piece, I saw a jagged piece of copper-colored satin sewn to the edge of the pelt. A coat. Someone had ripped, or torn up, a fur coat. And that same someone had attacked and killed Prucilla, breaking her dog show awards in the process.

"Lady!" Daisy exclaimed, pulling the phone from her ear as she looked frantically around the room. "Where's Lady?"

I looked around as well, noting the open crate door. "Hiding somewhere in the house, maybe? Playing in another room with the rest of the escaped puppies?" The ones Daisy and I had picked up, only to quickly put down when we'd discovered Prucilla, had run from the room and were busy chasing each other down the hall, barking happily as if there wasn't a dead woman lying in the living room in a pool of blood.

"We need to step into the hallway. Actually, we should wait on the front porch until the police come." I put down the pieces of fur, coming to my senses. This was a crime scene, and we were contaminating evidence. That, and I was suddenly very nervous that whoever had done this to Prucilla might still be in the house.

"But the puppies!" Three of them ran past the living room door as Daisy spoke. "We can't just leave the puppies running around. Or Lady."

I ushered my friend out of the living room, shutting the door behind me so the puppies couldn't get in. "I'm sure Prucilla has puppy-proofed her house, and the police will be here soon. Let's step onto the porch. We really shouldn't be in here right now."

Once outside, Daisy began to pace as sirens sounded in the distance.

"When did this happen?" she asked. "I just spoke to Prucilla a half hour ago. Who could have done this?"

"I don't know." Clearly she'd been murdered in the half an hour between her call with Daisy and when we'd arrived. Had the killer been here when she and Daisy had spoken? Daisy had said the woman seemed distracted, but with a new arrival from a hoarding situation, and with nine puppies to take care of, who *wouldn't* be distracted?

And where was Lady? How had all the puppies gotten out of the pen in the dining room? One had escaped before, but they *all* seemed to be running around this time. Had Prucilla set the puppies free while she made them dinner? Or had the killer done so?

"They're here!" Daisy dashed down the walkway to wave the first responders in. Police cars swarmed the quiet street, and neighbors began to come out of their houses to watch the commotion.

I moved to the side as two sheriff's deputies came up the walkway. "Be careful," I told them. "There are puppies running everywhere and a dog that's missing from her cage. I shut the living room door to keep them out. That's where she is…where we found her."

They went in and I moved farther down the walkway to stand next to Daisy. More police arrived. A van pulled up that I recognized as being from the Medical Examiner's office. It shook me to see it, to realize that Prucilla wouldn't be leaving in an ambulance, but in a zipped-up black bag in the back of a van. Dead. How could she be dead? We'd just seen her this morning. Daisy had just spoken to her a half an hour ago. We were here to fill out paperwork for Daisy to adopt Lady, and instead had found the scene of a murder.

"Ms. Kay? Ms. Daisy? Do you all have a moment?"

I recognized the voice and turned to see Miles Pickford standing behind me.

The deputy cleared his throat. "The detective will be here in just a moment. He's going to need to take a statement from the both of you."

"Oh. Of course." I frowned, wondering who was getting assigned to the case and fearing the worst.

"Detective Desmond Keeler," Miles told me with a wince.

That guy hated me, and I wasn't particularly fond of him either. But as much as I disliked Detective Keeler, the man was good at his job.

"There are puppies loose in the house," I told Miles.

"And a dog missing out of her cage," Daisy added.

"The officers will make sure they're safe," he assured us. "We've got two deputies inside securing the scene. We've got techs ready to go once they get the okay. There's an officer trying to get hold of the next of kin—a sister and a niece. And Detective Keeler is on his way."

My lips twitched. "And your job is…?"

He looked down at his feet. "Making sure you ladies aren't hurt. Keeping you here until the Detective arrives so he can talk to you."

"Making sure we don't muck anything up?" I teased.

Miles glanced up at me, and I swear he blushed. "Sorry,

Ms. Kay. The detective said he doesn't want you nosing around in things and messing up his case."

As I'd said, Detective Keeler hated me. I was a nosy busybody sticking my nose into police business, in his opinion. Of course he'd want someone babysitting me until he arrived.

Daisy and I stood in silence, waiting. Miles's radio squawked continually, and he occasionally answered it, barking out official sounding codes. I looked over to Daisy, who sighed.

"I wish they'd let us know if they've found Lady or not," she said.

Neither of us had seen the dog when we were inside, and we hadn't seen her outside either. She hadn't run out the front door when we'd arrived, but I was still worried that she'd somehow escaped not only her cage, but the house entirely.

"Was the back door open?" I asked Daisy. "Did you notice when we were in there?"

There had been a door off the kitchen to the backyard, then the French doors off the living room as well. I assumed they had been closed, or there probably would have been a draft from the chilly February air.

"I didn't notice the doors being open." Daisy's brow furrowed. "You don't think she got out, do you?"

"She has to be in the house somewhere," I reassured her, far from positive about that fact. "Maybe she's hiding upstairs under a bed?"

At that time, a gray Charger pulled up. It didn't have any badging, but from the mirrors, I could tell it was a police car. A tall, thin, clean-shaven black man wearing a dark suit exited the car and made his way toward us. Miles met him halfway, and they paused, exchanging a few words before the pair of them walked back toward us.

"I'm going to go in and check on things. Maybe help with the puppies and finding that missing dog," Miles said. "Detective Keeler here will take your statements."

Miles went into the house, and Detective Keeler took a pad of paper and a pen out of his pocket.

"How well do you both know Ms. Downing?" he asked. "Records show she lived alone. We've been trying to reach a sister and a niece over in Williamstown, but haven't got ahold of either yet. Do you ladies know if there's someone else we should be calling?"

"We only met her this morning," Daisy confessed. "I really don't know her personally."

"Me either." I added.

There was a noise at the door and we all glanced over. Two men were wheeling out a gurney with a black bag on top. I shivered, still hardly able to believe that the black bag held a woman we'd just been talking to this morning.

The detective sighed and put his pad of paper back in his pocket. "I need to ask you both to come down to the station to answer some questions."

"Are we arrested?" Daisy looked downright giddy at the prospect. I wasn't so excited.

"We weren't trespassing," I told the detective. "We didn't attack her. She runs an animal rescue. Daisy's putting an application in on one of her dogs. She was expecting us. She didn't answer the door when we knocked, but the puppies were all barking and we figured she didn't hear us, so we went in."

Keeler held up both hands. "I'm not arresting anyone—at least not yet. But I do need to ask you all some questions. It's darned cold to be standing outside like this, and the three of us squeezing into a police car isn't going to be much better."

"So you're taking us to the station." Daisy grinned with enthusiasm.

"I've been there before. It's not all that exciting," I told her.

"Are we going to be in the back of a squad car?" she asked. "Lights and sirens?"

Keeler sighed. "I'm in an unmarked car, and you don't have to ride with me—in fact, I'd prefer you didn't. You both can follow me to the station in your own cars. It's warm there and comfortable and you won't be standing in the cold outside the crime scene as we're working it."

"The police station is not that comfortable," I said to Daisy. "The chairs are hard and the coffee is never fresh."

"It's more comfortable than standing out here, practically in the street," Keeler argued. "And I promise I'll make some fresh coffee."

"What about the puppies?" Daisy asked. "Are you just going to leave them here in the house, alone? And Lady? What if she comes out of hiding and everyone's gone and she's in the house with a bunch of puppies? Alone. Scared."

Keeler looked as if he wanted to be anywhere but here right now. "We're trying to get ahold of the sister or the niece. Hopefully one of them will come to take care of the dogs, but I guess I should just call animal control."

That was the wrong thing to say. Daisy erupted into hand-waving distress, telling him the pups were too young to go to the shelter, that locking them up in a cold, cement-floor cage in a noisy place would do irreparable damage to their young psyches. I didn't point out that we'd just come from the shelter not three hours ago where the cement-floor cages had comfy dog beds and blankets and there was a separate, quieter area for animals who'd just arrived. Daisy was on a roll, advocating for the welfare of these rescue pups, and I wasn't about to stop her.

"We call animal control." The detective glared at Daisy. "That's what we do. It's procedure."

"I'm sure they'll take good care of the animals," I said to

my friend, trying to reassure her. It didn't work.

"We're taking the puppies," Daisy announced. "And Lady, if I can find her. I'll just go inside and look through the house—"

"No, you won't," Keeler snapped. "This is a *crime scene*, ma'am. You can't go inside. You can't go searching the house, and you can't go taking things out of it either—even if those things are puppies and a dog."

My friend fixed him with a hard stare. "I'm taking those puppies. *And* Lady, once we find her."

Keeler glared at her. "I won't let you take anything from a crime scene. I'm gonna call animal control. That's procedure. That's how things are done."

Thankfully, at that point, Miles and an officer exited the house. Keeler walked over to speak with the officer, and Miles made his way toward us, breaking the tension.

"The puppies are safe and all in the penned in area," he announced. "We've searched the house and there's no other dog there. I'm sorry, but I think the dog might have gotten out during the course of the murder."

"No!" Daisy took a step forward. "Where is she? It's cold. It's going to be dark soon. I can't leave until she's found."

"She was coming to fill out papers to adopt that dog," I told Miles, trying to explain why Daisy was so distraught.

"The puppies! We're not leaving the puppies here. I'm going in to get them, and I'm not going to the police station until we find Lady."

"I'm sure one of the neighbors has the dog," Miles tried to assure her. "If she got out, then she probably ran over to someone else's place, and they took her to the shelter. And we'll call animal control to take the puppies."

"*I'm* taking those puppies," Daisy insisted.

The deputy stepped in front of her. "No, you're not. I can't let you in there, Ms. Daisy. I can't let some random woman enter a crime scene and take things out of a house that don't even belong to her."

"Miles Pickford," Daisy spluttered. "I'm *not* a random woman. I've known you since you were in diapers. I was in ninth grade biology with your mother."

She was? But this was no time to quiz my friend on Miles's mother and ninth grade biology class. There was about to be a standoff between Daisy and the law, and I needed to diffuse the situation before my friend really did end up cuffed and riding to the station in the back of a squad car with lights and sirens on.

"You've volunteered at the shelter," I reminded Daisy. "I'm sure they'd let you foster the puppies until Prucilla's sister or niece gets up here. *And* Lady. They probably have Lady right now, and if they don't she's snug in one of the neighbor's garage's, eating their cat food."

Daisy muttered something about making a few phone calls, then stomped down the walkway to her car. I turned to Miles with an apologetic smile.

"I'm sorry. She's so upset. She's worried about Lady being missing. She's worried about the puppies." I waved a hand toward the front door. "And we're both upset about finding Prucilla like this. We might not have known her very well, but she was kind and clearly devoted to the animals in her rescue. Daisy feels like she has an obligation to make sure those animals don't slip through the cracks right now. And so do I."

Miles nodded, his stance relaxing. "I know. But the shelter will take good care of the animals, and we'll find the person who killed Prucilla Downing. Keeler's a good detective."

"I know he is." I reached out and patted the deputy's arm. What I didn't tell him was that I planned on doing everything I could to help the good Detective find the killer.

$\mathcal{I}$ drove us to the station because Daisy needed to be on the phone the whole time, making arrangements with the animal shelter to temporarily foster the puppies. After we parked, I sent a quick text off to Judge Beck, telling him I was going to be late and not to hold dinner for me.

Once again, crime was interfering with my plans. I felt a bit silly wishing that murders and assaults and other nefarious deeds would happen neatly between the hours of nine-to-five on weekdays, allowing for an hour midday for lunch. Criminals didn't keep bankers' hours, and crime disrupted plans and lives. It was horrible of me to be regretting a missed dinner with the Judge when Prucilla had just been murdered. My life may have been slightly disrupted, my plans inconvenience, but her life had been shoved off a cliff.

A shadow materialized beside the car, following Daisy and me as we made our way into the police station. Prucilla's ghost had stayed with her body when Daisy and I had gone outside, and I hadn't seen it again until just now. Its presence was one more reminder that someone had lost their life today.

Prucilla Downing's spirit needed my assistance. I got the impression the ghost was concerned about more than bringing her killer to justice, too. I hoped that something Daisy and I saw or heard would help the detective find whoever had killed the woman, but I knew I wouldn't allow my part in this to end at the station. I'd do what I could to help solve her murder. And while I was doing that, Daisy would make sure the puppies were taken care of and that Lady was found.

Detective Keeler escorted us into a cramped interview room with uncomfortable chairs, beige walls, and a linoleum floor that looked as if it had been installed in the sixties. The ghost hovered in a corner beside the door. Keeler left, and by the time he'd returned about five minutes later with three cups of coffee, the ghost was gone.

I took a tentative sip of my coffee, then smiled over at him. "Thank you."

"Not a problem. I wanted a fresh cup myself." The detective sat opposite us and arranged a notepad on the table, as well as a recording device.

The coffee was weak and there were a few grounds floating in it, but it was fresh. I'd take weak with floaties any day over the usual sludge that looked and tasted like it had been in the coffee pot for six to twelve hours.

Keeler turned the recorder on, then went through the usual spiel, identifying himself as well as us and the matter at hand.

"So." He clicked his pen and moved it to hover over the pad of paper. "What were the pair of you were doing at Prucilla Downing's house?"

Daisy jumped right in. "I'm looking to adopt a dog. Her rescue was recommended, and I'd sent her a quick e-mail last night expressing interest in a few dogs she had available. She invited me to come by this morning to talk about the dogs and the adoption process. Kay and I were there about ten o'clock this morning."

Keeler made notes while Daisy and I outlined our visit. My friend waxed poetic about Lady, then I told the detective about the puppy escape, and how Prucilla had said they were little Houdinis.

"But the pen was opened this afternoon," I pointed out. "I saw it. The puppies were running around, so I glanced into the room as we went inside. They hadn't escaped this time. Someone folded up the pen wall and let them out. Whether Prucilla had done it, or someone else had, I don't know."

"But why would a killer let the puppies loose?" Daisy asked no one in particular. "It doesn't seem like there's any reason to do that."

"Maybe to mess up the crime scene?" I shrugged. "Plus, I don't think the killer broke in or anything. There was no sign of anyone smashing a window or forcing the door open. I think Prucilla knew her attacker and actually let him, or her, into the house."

"The door *was* unlocked," Daisy pointed out. "The killer could have just walked on in."

"Wait, wait." Keeler waved his hands at us. "Hold on now. Let's keep all that for the end of this interview. I'm trying to get a sense of a timeline here."

"Sorry." I sat back, trying to listen to his questions, but I kept thinking about the door. Had it been locked when we'd come early this morning? I frowned, picturing it all in my mind. We'd arrived. Knocked. Prucilla had opened the door. I couldn't remember if she'd had to unlock it or not. Maybe she was just a person who always left her door unlocked.

No. If I had a bunch of rescue puppies that kept escaping their pen and a brand-new rescue dog who might bolt from her cage and never been seen again, I'd keep my doors locked. It wasn't a matter of security or fear of robbery, but more a fear that a friendly neighbor or prospective adopter might accidentally let the dogs out.

We went on to tell the detective about the rest of our day —the visits to the shelters and other rescues, our quick lunch at the new bistro in Milford, and our narrowing down of the candidates for Daisy's new four-legged best friend.

"I'd called Prucilla about a half an hour before we arrived to let her know I wanted to put in an application on Lady— the one that's missing from the cage in the living room," Daisy told the detective. "She said to come on by, so we drove there. When we arrived, we knocked, but no one answered. We didn't hear anyone inside except the dogs. They were barking like crazy." Daisy's eyes lit up. "Wait! I heard Lady barking. It wasn't just puppies. There was a grown dog barking in the house, and Lady was the only adult dog in the place. She's *got* to be there somewhere."

I put a hand on Daisy's shoulder before she could jump to her feet and dash out of the station. "If she's in the house somewhere, hiding, the police will find her. Or animal control will when they get there for the puppies."

Daisy let out a long breath. "Right. I made some calls, and if the sister or niece can't be there to take care of the dogs, then I can foster them. If Lady's there hiding, they'll find her and I'll pick her up with the puppies."

"So you knocked and heard the dogs..." Keeler prodded.

Ugh. Here's where we looked like trespassers. Although it was a good thing we'd gone on in the house, otherwise who knew how long Prucilla would have lain there, dead on the living room floor.

"Prucilla was expecting us," I repeated. "We figured she might not hear us knocking with all the racket, and that maybe she was getting dinner for the dogs in the back somewhere, so we opened the door a crack and called out that we were there."

"And then?" Keeler asked.

Daisy explained that we'd opened the door wider, that there were puppies running by, and that we'd gone in just to help corral them. It was totally trespassing, but Prucilla had been running a non-profit business out of her house and we'd been invited, so hopefully that didn't *really* count as trespassing where the police were concerned.

"What exactly did you see and hear at that point? This is really important," Detective Keeler said.

"I grabbed a puppy and ran after another into the living room," I told him. "When I saw Prucilla on the floor, and all the blood, I immediately dropped the puppy and checked her for a heartbeat."

"I'd picked up a puppy and gone after Kay. She told me to call 911, so I put the puppy down and called for help. Then we left, shutting the door so the puppies couldn't get into the room and went back outside to wait for the police to arrive."

I closed my eyes, thinking back to that moment, picturing it in my mind. "When I found her, Prucilla was wearing the same clothes she'd had on that morning. All the trophies from the mantel were laying broken on the floor a few feet from her. One had blood on it—I assumed it was the weapon the killer used. And there was a bunch of chunks of fur strewn around. I wondered what it was and picked a piece up. I think it was from a fur coat? While I was doing that, Daisy was on the phone with 911, and the puppies were still barking and running around the hallway. But I didn't hear Lady at that time, just the puppies."

"You're right!" Daisy exclaimed. "I hadn't heard her since we came in either, although I'm sure I heard a grown dog barking when we were knocking on the door."

"And the puppy pen was opened, not knocked over," I

added. "The house smelled like puppies and coffee. Fresh coffee." I looked down into my cup. "I don't know if she'd made it for us, knowing we were on our way, or someone else."

"We'll check the pot and any cups in the sink or elsewhere in the house," Keeler said. "Is there anything else you can remember?"

I frowned, thinking that there was something just at the edge of my memories—at the edge and slightly out of reach. "Not now, but I'll be sure to let you know if something else comes to mind."

He nodded, then ended the recording and shut off the device. "Thank you both for your time. I'll be in touch."

I knew a dismissal when I heard one. The detective didn't like me. He thought I was a snoopy old lady, always underfoot in his cases. He wasn't wrong, but that didn't mean I was going to give the man any slack. I liked to know what was going on, to help out when I could. I was a private investigator now, after all. But with Detective Keeler on the case, I'd be lucky if I read about any updates in the paper.

Maybe I could rely on Miles to fill me in. I'd be making a whole lot of muffins and scones this week as bribes to get information out of the deputy. He always liked baked goods.

And if that didn't work, I'd ask Violet. She worked at the courthouse. Plus, she and Miles had been dating, and I knew the deputy would confide in her.

It all felt so surreal. We'd spent the day looking at cute dogs and catching up on gossip. It wasn't supposed to end like this. And Prucilla...she'd seemed so nice.

You'd think after having come across so many murder victims in the last year that seeing Prucilla on the floor wouldn't have left me stunned and confused, but it never got easy. I didn't think it would ever get easy.

"Have they cleared the crime scene yet?" Daisy asked.

"Did they find Lady? Did someone get in touch with Prucilla's sister, or niece?"

The detective hesitated before speaking, as if he was undecided how much information to disclose to us. "The niece is on her way here. Animal control has the puppies, and the niece said she can't take them 'cause of her apartment lease or something. There wasn't any other dog, or person, or anything in the house. Just the victim and the puppies."

Daisy sucked in a breath. "Where did Lady go? She didn't run past us, and I shut the door when I came in. If she's not in the house, then where is she?"

I shivered, because if Lady had gotten out of the house, then someone had let her out between the time we'd knocked and when we'd entered the house. Had we really been that close to witnessing a crime? To interrupting the murder of Prucilla Downing? If we'd arrived moments earlier, would she be alive and not in dead right now?

Who'd killed Prucilla Downing? And, assuming it was the same person, who'd let the dog out?

CHAPTER 6

*D*aisy was quiet and distracted as she drove me home. She told me she'd see me in the morning for yoga, then backed out of the drive while I climbed onto the porch. I noticed she didn't turn left to head to her house, but instead turned right, heading back into town.

I watched her go, my heart aching for my friend. Daisy would pick up the puppies either tonight or tomorrow. Then she'd look for Lady. My friend wouldn't give up until the dog was found and was safe. She'd spend all day tomorrow talking to neighbors, walking the subdivision, putting up flyers and calling dog-finding-dog trackers.

And I'd be right there with her.

Taco greeted me at the door and I scooped the cat into my arms, heading for the kitchen. The aroma of roast chicken had filled my nose as soon as I'd walked in, and I felt guilty for missing dinner.

I felt worse when I walked into the room and saw two plates set on the center island with actual cloth napkins under the silverware and a vase full of pink carnations flanked by two candles. The basement stairs creaked, and Judge Beck appeared.

"I'm so sorry," I told him. "You must be starved. I feel terrible that you waited for me."

"I had a snack." He took Taco from me and plopped the cat down on the floor. "Sit. I'll get the chicken out of the oven."

This was not how I wanted to start off a relationship with him. "I'm not normally so late. When I make a commitment, I keep it. I honestly couldn't get here in time. I'm so sorry."

"It's all right, Kay."

He got the chicken out of the oven and I winced, worried that it might be dry and tough as shoe leather at this point. But it looked fine as he took the foil off and set the roasting pan on some potholders in front of the two plates.

I grabbed a grill lighter from one of the kitchen drawers and lit the candles. It might not be the romantic dinner he'd planned, but I'd do what I could to try to salvage this evening.

The judge motioned for me to sit, then turned to pull a salad and some wine from the fridge. "So, tell me about your day. I'm guessing Daisy found a dog she liked? And that the application process took longer than expected?"

Oh sheesh. I'd forgotten to tell him! In the text I'd first sent, I'd only told him I wouldn't be home on time, and the second one I'd sent as we were leaving the station just said we were on our way.

If my lateness hadn't already put a dent in the romantic vibe of the evening, then my tale of murder definitely would.

I settled into my chair, holding my glass out as Judge Beck poured the wine. "Yes, Daisy found a dog she wanted to adopt, but when we got back to the woman's house, we found her dead on the floor. Murdered." I told him what had happened, and he stared, dinner momentarily forgotten.

"Kay, that's terrible!" Judge Beck frowned. "You and Daisy must have gotten there right after the attack. You could have walked in on it."

I went to tell him that I thought between the two of us, Daisy and I could manage to fend off a trophy-wielding killer, but realized I had no way of knowing if one person had murdered Prucilla Downing, or if she'd been attacked by several people. There had only been a half an hour between when Daisy had spoken to her on the phone and we'd arrived. That wasn't much time to get inside, hit Prucilla over the head, then trash the place. There were a lot of trophies and plaques to break, and those furs couldn't have been easy to cut up. Judge Beck was right, we probably *had* arrived just after the killer, or killers, were leaving.

Daisy had said she remembered hearing Lady's bark, then not hearing Lady's bark. Had we interrupted the murderer and he'd fled out the back just as we were coming in the front door? If we hadn't arrived just then, what would he have done? Trashed the house further? Hurt the puppies? Was he looking for something, or was his intent only to kill Prucilla? And where was Lady? I hoped the dog had just escaped when the killer left because it terrified me to think he might have taken the dog with him and hurt her as he'd hurt Prucilla.

"Broken dog show trophies and slashed fur coats? That sounds like radical activists." Judge Beck lifted a brow. "Or people who want the police to *think* the murderers are radical activists."

I hadn't really had time to think about the details of the crime, what with Daisy's concern over Lady and the puppies, and the questioning at the police station, but Judge Beck was right. I sipped my wine and thought while he filled two bowls with salad and sat down beside me.

"What do we know about Prucilla Downing?" I mused as I

took a bite of salad. He'd gone all out, adding in bits of olives, salami, cheese, and cucumbers to the standard lettuce-and-tomato mix. I was pretty sure the dressing was homemade too, and not out of a bottle.

"Prucilla Downing?" Judge Beck asked. "Well, according to your friends, she runs a rescue and is very vocal and active in attempting to shut down puppy mills."

"How long did she have the rescue business?" I grabbed my phone and started to Google. "The broken trophies on the floor had been on the mantel when Daisy and I got there this morning. Evidently she'd once bred and shown Boxers."

"Olive said that lots of breeders get into the rescue business, although they tend to stick to breed-specific rescue," Judge Beck commented. "Maybe Prucilla started with Boxer rescue, then moved to mix breeds."

"Her website doesn't say anything about that, but it does say Second Chance was founded eleven years ago." I alternated bites of salad with scrolling and found something interesting. "Four years ago is when I'm seeing pictures of a wide variety of dogs. Before then, they look to be mostly Boxers, Boxer-mixes, and some bull-breed mixes."

"So, who would want Prucilla Downing dead?" Judge Beck pulled the chicken toward him and started to carve it.

"I don't know her well enough to answer that question. For all I know, there's an angry ex-husband out there, or a long-standing feud with a family member, or even a neighbor she's been fighting with." Finishing my salad, I moved the bowl aside.

If I'd learned anything in the past year, it was that small slights could, over time, add up and escalate to violence. But what happened to Prucilla seemed like it was more than just an argument that got out of hand. I could envision someone grabbing a trophy off the mantel and hitting Prucilla with it in a moment of fury, but breaking all the trophies and throwing them on the floor? Slicing up a fur coat and throwing it down beside a dead woman? That felt like it was more than something done in a moment of fury. It felt as if it might be premeditated.

"Did Prucilla even *have* a fur coat?" I thought out loud. "Or did her killer bring that with him or her? She really didn't seem like the fur coat type."

Judge Beck placed some chicken on my plate before serving himself. "You're the private investigator here. Let's throw out some potential motives and see what we've got."

"Outside of the possible angry ex, relative, or neighbor?" I held up my hands. "Prucilla worked to shut down that puppy mill. That's a motive."

Judge Beck nodded. "Or maybe she refused a potential adopter?"

"Ooo, that's a good one." I dug around in the island drawer for a pad of paper and a pen, then wrote down both ideas.

"It *could* be activists," the judge pointed out. "Maybe they think she's a hypocrite because she used to breed and show, or they think she's not going far enough and needs to condemn all breeders instead of just puppy mills."

"Seems like a shaky motive," I mused. "She's still doing good on behalf of animal welfare. I can't imagine someone would want to kill her for not doing enough." I wrote it down anyway.

"I don't know. I've had more than a few assault cases in my courtroom with those Free the Fur people," he commented.

I winced, remembering that last year members of the group had been arrested for throwing paint on everyone with leather and fur coats at the shopping mall. Ironically, some of the people they'd assaulted had been wearing fake fur and fake leather. Then at Christmas, they'd taken to protesting the horse-drawn carriage rides in downtown Milford, harassing potential customers and causing such a scene that the carriage company stopped offering the rides. But harassment and assault were a far cry from murder.

Or were they? I remembered in college where groups were sometimes whipped into a frenzy, and how quickly a peaceful demonstration could turn violent. Maybe Free the Fur had an issue with Prucilla, and a longstanding disagreement had escalated. A confrontation in the living room. Yelling, and smashing trophies. A sliced-up coat. A struggle where Prucilla tried to grab the trophies or coat away from the other person. Then a heat-of-the-moment, deadly assault, followed by a frantic dash out the back door when Daisy and I had started knocking. If that had been the case, they'd probably left tons of evidence behind for the police.

It was plausible, but it didn't seem to fit for some reason. I still made a note on my paper before flipping to a clean sheet.

"I'm just writing a few things down," I told the judge, feeling guilty that my overcooked chicken was now growing cold. "Facts, and things I should look into a bit further." I smiled over at him. "Things I should look into as a nosy woman, that is, because I haven't been hired to investigate this and I'm obviously not a police detective."

"Nosy women need answers too." He smiled back.

"Yes we do," I agreed.

"Okay then. We've got smashed dog show trophies," he counted off on his fingers. "Puppies intentionally released from the pen. A dog missing not only from a secure cage, but from the house. A sliced-up fur coat. An unlocked front door."

"I'm going to look into applications that have been turned down in the last few months," I scribbled frantically on the pad. "And any puppy mills or rescues or shelters or breeders that Prucilla has criticized or been instrumental in getting shut down or fined. I'll look into the background on the puppies, and the hoarder situation that Lady came from, in case that was a factor in Prucilla's murder. I'll check Prucilla's history with any of the animal activist groups including Free the Fur." I bit the end of my pen and looked at the judge. "Do you think I should check out her dog show and breeding history with the Boxers? Seems like if that had been a contributing factor, then it would have come up four or more years ago, not now."

"Sometimes stuff from the past bubbles up to the surface," he said. "I've had cases where something that happened a decade ago was the spark that started a fight that ended in a stabbing. Maybe she beat someone out of a big dog show win a decade ago, and that person's anger and hatred has been stewing ever since."

I nodded. "One trigger, and they're driving over to Prucilla's, ready to smash her trophies and hit her over the head with one. But then why the fur coat?"

The judge held up his hands. "To make it look like the activists did it? A panicked attempt to cover his or her tracks once they realized that they might have murdered someone?"

I knew this probably wasn't the romantic dinner Judge Beck had hoped for, but sitting here over cold, overcooked chicken, discussing a case, I found myself falling more and more for him. This was something we bonded over. This was something we were both passionate about. Was it weird that a romance was being built on a shared love for justice?

"I'm sorry I was late," I told him again. "I'd been looking forward to this all day, but the murder...and then the police wanted a statement. Desmond Keeler is the detective on the case, and he's not a man anyone says no to."

He smiled, and this time there wasn't any lingering hurt in his expression. "It's fine. You texted to let me know. And I'm pretty sure Detective Keeler wouldn't have accepted prior dinner plans as a reason to decline his invitation to the station."

I laughed. "Actually, he would have if I'd told him the dinner plans were with you. Judge Beck's name gets all the law enforcement folks to jump. I don't like to name drop, though."

His smile widened. "No, you wouldn't. Not even to get out of a speeding ticket."

"Well, for a speeding ticket, I might." I laughed.

We ate in silence for a bit. The chicken was good. But even with dinner and the judge by my side, my thoughts kept returning to the earlier events of the evening.

"Miles Pickford was one of the Deputies on the scene," I told the judge. "He's such a nice young man. He went inside to make sure the other officers had corralled up and contained the puppies, and to see if they'd found Lady. He was so helpful, even with Daisy on the edge of getting herself arrested."

Judge Beck snorted out a laugh. "Daisy? Arrested?"

"She was worried about leaving the puppies there with no one home, and then there was the missing dog." I sighed. "Lady is the dog she was going to adopt. We heard her barking when we were at the door, but she was nowhere to be found once we got inside. Daisy wanted to search the house, then take Lady and the puppies home with her until Prucilla's niece or someone showed up to take care of them, but Keeler and Miles wouldn't let her in the house. Things were getting heated, and I didn't think Daisy was going to back down. She was so upset."

"The procedure is to call animal control?" Judge Beck sipped his wine as I nodded. "They would make sure the animals were safe and taken care of. As for Lady, the police would have swept the premises to make sure the intruder wasn't hiding somewhere. If there was a dog under a bed upstairs, I'm sure they would have found it."

"I know. But Daisy was so distraught. I'm sure she went back there after dropping me off to see if the neighbors had seen Lady running around, or if the dog was hiding in the backyard. The whole way to the police station she was on the phone with the shelter, arranging to foster the puppies and Lady."

"Poor Daisy must be beside herself with worry." Judge Beck stood to gather up our plates.

"She is," I agreed.

My friend and I had left this morning, looking forward to a day filled with adorable dogs. We'd headed back to Prucilla's this afternoon with every intention of her adopting Lady, and now the dog was missing. Had she broken out of her cage and run off? How had she managed to get out of the house? The front door had been closed, although not locked, when we arrived, and I was sure I would have noticed a draft if the back door had been left open. Someone had either taken the dog, or let her out as they fled out the back door. The police would be looking for Prucilla's assailant, but would anyone be looking for Lady? Besides Daisy, that was?

"I think that my nosy-woman sleuthing is going to have to take a backseat to helping Daisy." I got up to assist Judge Beck with the leftovers and dishes. "I'm going to spend tomorrow putting up flyers and knocking on doors with her, trying to see if we can track down the missing dog. I'm hoping one of the neighbors saw Lady and has her safely in their garage, because Daisy is not going to give up until that dog is found."

"Let me know if I can help," he told me. "I've got a little work to do in the morning, but then I'm free until Heather brings the kids over at five. I'm more than willing to knock on doors, hang up flyers, and tromp through the woods looking for Daisy's dog."

Daisy's dog. The thought made me smile. I might be worried, well aware that Lady's story could have a tragic ending, but I didn't want to think about that. I'd rather hope that a neighbor had the dog warm and safe in a garage, and that tomorrow Daisy could bring her new four-legged-best-friend home.

Judge Beck and I put the food away, loaded the dishwasher, and were just about to take our glasses of wine downstairs for a movie when the doorbell rang. I exchanged a puzzled glance with the judge and set my wine on the table as I went to answer the door. It was after ten o'clock, and while that wasn't exactly midnight, good news generally didn't arrive late in the evening—especially on a weekend.

I swung the door open to see my friend Daisy standing on the porch, four crates stuffed full of loud boisterous puppies at her feet.

Puppies, but no adult dog.

"Have you heard anything about Lady?" I asked her, my heart pounding with fear at what her answer might be.

"No. No good news, but no bad news either. She's not anywhere around the outside of the house. The police said they didn't find her inside the home. One neighbor said he thought he saw a dog running across his back yard this evening, but he's not positive. The good news is that no one has reported a traffic accident involving a dog, and I didn't see her body on the side of any of the roads within a few miles of Prucilla's house."

"Oh, Daisy." My heart ached for my friend. "We'll find her. Judge Beck and I will help you look for her tomorrow. We'll find her, I promise." And hopefully the dog would be alive and unhurt when we did.

"Thank you. I really appreciate the help. I'm going to use

the picture I took of her this morning and make up some flyers to post around tomorrow. But Kay…" Daisy grimaced. "I hate to ask you this. I need a favor. A big favor."

"Anything," I promised. If she needed me to research something, make some phone calls, or to just use my printer for the flyers, I'd do it. I said I'd do anything for my friend, and I meant it.

But I wasn't quite prepared for the favor Daisy was about to ask.

"There are nine puppies, and I just can't…" She looked down at the cages. "It's too many for me to handle. I haven't had a dog in ages, let alone a puppy—let alone *nine* puppies. I don't want them to go to the shelter, and I made a commitment to take care of them. But I didn't realize how over my head I was until I picked them up from animal control. Can you take half of them? Please? Just until another rescue can take them in or other fosters are found?"

I stared down at the little squirming furry balls in the cages and gulped. Five puppies. Or four, because half would be four-and-a-half puppies, and Daisy clearly wasn't going to do a King Solomon and split the litter in half literally. I'd never had a puppy, hadn't had a dog since I was a child. The only experience I had was with Taco, who I'd adopted as a fully grown cat less than a year ago.

But Daisy was my best friend, so I did what a person did when their best friend needed them. I said yes.

CHAPTER 7

*J*udge Beck helped me get the two cages of puppies into the house. We papered the floor of the downstairs powder room, filled bowls with water and some of the food Daisy had left with us, then blocked the doorway with the cages. Four puppies jumped and raced around the small area while we looked on. One tried to climb up the side of the toilet. Another grabbed the end of the toilet paper and ran. Others joined in to attack the streamer of TP, ripping it apart.

"Oh no you don't!" I climbed in and removed the toilet paper from the roll, placing it safely in the under-sink cabinet. At least, I hoped it was safe there. Maybe I needed to get child-proof locks on the cabinet. In the meantime I removed anything that might be toxic or a choking hazard and handed it out to Judge Beck to store safely away in the kitchen, out of what had temporarily become the puppy zone.

Then Judge Beck climbed into the powder room with me and we began cleaning up the shredded toilet paper mess. It was a tight fit, and one wrong turn had me tripping over the food bowl and pitching straight into his arms.

He held me for a second, and I made no effort to free myself.

"I think we're in for a long night." His voice was husky and deep, and I caught my breath, my mind immediately going to thoughts of the two of us doing things I wasn't sure I was ready for us to do.

Then I realized he meant the puppies.

"Oh! Yes, we probably are." I laughed and stepped away from him to pick one of the little guys up. "Should we name them? If we don't, you know Madison and Henry will."

"Which means they'll end up being named Beyoncé or Jay-Z or something," he said ruefully.

"So as a preemptive assertion of our age and culture, we should name them James Taylor and Carly Simon?" I turned the puppy I was holding to get a better look at his undercarriage. "Say hello to James?"

He took the pup from my hands. "Doesn't look like a James to me. I'm a judge. You're a private investigator. Let's name them something more in line with our professions."

"You're not seriously going to name that little guy after Chief Justice John Roberts? How is John any better than James?"

I bent to pick up the other puppies one at a time and checked their gender. Two boys, including the one Judge Beck held, and two girls.

Judge Beck lifted the pup he was holding to his face where it squirmed and licked his hands. They were all of indeterminant parentage with short velvety fur, huge pointy ears, and long snouts. The one the judge held was white with black ticking and a large black spot covering the left side of his face. The other boy was solid black. The two girls were brown, one with a black mask and black ears. I picked the solid brown girl up, noting a spot of white on her chin.

"Starsky and Hutch," Judge Beck announced.

I laughed. "Were you even born when that show was on?"

"I think I was born the year it started," he confessed. "But I've seen the reruns, and they did do a film remake about thirty years later."

"With Ben Stiller and Owen Wilson." I loved the detective shows of my youth, and sometimes even the cheesy, not-so-good remakes. "Snoop Dogg as Huggy Bear was the best thing about that movie."

"Snoop Dogg is the best thing about every movie he's in." Judge Beck stroked the puppy. "Maybe we should name one Huggy Bear as well."

"There's two boys and two girls, so that's a no. Starsky and Hutch it is. I'm assuming you're holding Hutch? And the solid black boy is Starsky?"

"Perfect. Right Hutch? What do you think about that?" The pup lunged forward and licked the judge's face.

I was going to explode from all this cuteness. Plus, a handsome man cuddling a puppy was incredibly sexy.

"Your turn," the judge told me. "You get to name the two girls."

"Cagney and Lacey," I immediately replied. "Since we're going with a 70's detective show theme here. This solid brown girl is Lacey and the other one is Cagney."

That done we finished our attempts to puppy-proof the powder room, then headed downstairs to watch our movie in the basement family room.

It had only been thirty minutes into the movie, and I'd already paused it four times to go check on the puppies who sounded as if they were destroying the powder room. Finally we gave up and brought the four of them downstairs with us, hoping some cuddle time on the couch would lull them to sleep.

No such luck. They squirmed out of our arms, chewed on the couch and the end tables. One pooped on the floor right in front of the television. Giving up on the movie, we cleaned up the mess, then headed upstairs, trying once more to get the puppies to settle down in the powder room before escaping to bed.

By the time my alarm went off at six in the morning, I figured I'd probably gotten about two hours of sleep in total. The puppies whined and yipped and howled. I got up every hour to check on them and make sure they hadn't somehow managed to open the toilet lid and fall in, or push the crates aside to run through the house. Daisy must have had a similar experience, as there was a text on my phone cancelling this morning's yoga and telling me she'd be by around eight with flyers.

Still in my pajamas, I fed Taco, commiserating with the frazzled cat. "They won't be here long," I assured him as I started the coffee. "Once Prucilla's niece arrives, she'll arrange for foster care or for another rescue to take them in, and they'll be gone."

I peeked around the corner to see the puppies finally sleeping in an adorable pile of fur amid torn newspaper and a shredded throw rug. What the heck was Daisy's plan for these little guys if Prucilla's family was too overwhelmed to deal with the dead woman's rescue and all these puppies? They looked to be around eight or nine weeks old. Should we be taking applications for their adoption? Actively searching for forever homes for them? Did the county shelter actually have ownership for the puppies, or was all that in limbo until Prucilla's next of kin arrived?

The stairs creaked, and I glanced up to see Judge Beck coming down. He was still in his pajamas as well, his hair messed, his eyes tired.

"I'm thinking we need to pick up some ear plugs for tonight," I commented.

He paused by the powder room. *"Now*, they're asleep. I was beginning to wonder if they would ever settle down."

"Me too." I covered a yawn. "I'm making coffee, and there's that leftover pumpkin spice loaf for breakfast. Yoga's cancelled for this morning. Daisy texted that she'll be over here at eight, so if you want to grab an extra hour of sleep, now's your chance."

"I'm awake now. Might as well stay awake and get some of my work done," he grumbled, and headed into the kitchen.

I bit back a smile, thinking how cute Judge Beck was sleep deprived and grumpy. The smell of coffee wafted out from the kitchen, and I heard the clink of the cups.

"What are we going to do with the puppies while we're out hanging up flyers and looking for Lady?" Judge Beck asked.

I hadn't really thought about that. We certainly couldn't leave them in the powder room unattended, and I didn't feel right having them locked in the cages for the whole day.

"I guess we'll take them with us? We could load the cages into the back of your SUV and maybe swing by a pet store for harnesses and leashes?"

The puppies had little color-coded collars, but I wouldn't trust those to hold if they tried to run off. Harnesses would be better. Maybe having the puppies trot along with us as we looked for Lady would wear them out so they'd sleep better tonight.

Judge Beck walked back into the hallway and handed me a mug of coffee. "I doubt they're leash trained at this age. We'll probably end up having to carry them around."

Ugh. So much for wearing the pups out. It seemed more likely *we'd* be the ones worn out. Maybe we'd be exhausted enough to sleep through all the noise tonight.

We enjoyed our coffee and pumpkin spice loaf in quiet,

then Daisy woke the puppies up into a frenzy of barking with a knock on the door.

"Oh my." She wrinkled her nose at the noise as I let her in. "I'm guessing you probably got as little sleep as I did last night."

"Where are your five little banshees?" I peeked past her to her car parked in the driveway.

"In their cages in the back seat of my car. I'm dropping them off at J.T.'s before I head out to look for Lady. He said he'd watch them for an hour or two, then I'll need to pick them up again."

I waved her in, shutting the door against the morning chill. "Do you think J.T. would mind watching our four, too?"

She laughed. "Right. I'll be lucky if I have a boyfriend after today. He wasn't happy about this. I'm going to owe him big time."

Wonderful. I guess the judge and I were just going to have to take the pups with us. Too bad Madison and Henry didn't arrive until tonight, or we could leave them in the kids' capable, and probably enthusiastic, hands.

"Come into the kitchen and have some coffee," I offered as the puppies settled down from barking to whining and yipping.

"Oh, I can't. I really want to get out there." Daisy handed me a huge stack of papers. "Here are the flyers. And here's the map. Prucilla's house is right there, with the X. I drew circles where each of us are going to be searching today. You and Judge Beck are taking the blue circle."

I blinked in surprise at the organization. "There are six circles, and just three of us."

"I enlisted help." Daisy rubbed a hand over her eyes. "Olive. Suzette. Kat. Violet Smith."

"We'll find her, Daisy." I patted my friend on the shoulder, then took the stack from her. "She might have even come back to Prucilla's house sometime in the night."

Daisy nodded. "I left a note on the door last night just in case Prucilla's niece or sister came by the house. I'm hoping they did. If Lady came back, and one of them was there, maybe they let her in."

"If not, then maybe one of the neighbors took her in."

Daisy sighed. "I hope so. It got cold last night, and I was so worried. Text me if you find anything out, or hear something, and I'll communicate with the rest of the group. Otherwise today is mostly hanging up flyers and asking around the neighborhood if anyone's seen her. I've got an appointment with a dog-tracker later this afternoon. If we haven't found her by then, I'm hoping he can. He came highly recommended."

"You sure you don't want a cup of coffee for the road?" I offered as she went to leave.

"I'm fine, thanks." She paused with her hand on the doorknob. "I appreciate your help today, Kay. You and the judge. Both of you."

I waved my friend off, then cleaned the mess in the powder room while Judge Beck got dressed. We swapped places, and he got the puppies in their cages, loading them, the flyers, and a supply of water and food into the SUV while I got ready. Before heading to our designated search area, we stopped off at the local pet store and I waited in the car with the puppies while he went inside.

"You guys sure are cute, but you're way too much for me to handle," I told the puppies. "I think I'm going to stick to cats—adult cats. Actually, I'm going to stick with one adult cat."

It wasn't long before the judge returned with several bags. It was clear from their size that the items stuffed inside weren't just leashes and halters.

"What the heck did you buy?" I took the bags from him as he got into the car.

"Leashes, harnesses. More food and treats." He gave me a sheepish grin. "Toys."

"Toys?" I looked inside and saw all sorts of things. Balls. Puppy pee pads. Chew sticks. Rubber Kongs and an assortment of treats and things to stuff inside them. "Um, you do realize that we might only have these puppies for another day or two? Or less if Prucilla's family has arrived. Technically, they belong to the rescue."

Maybe we shouldn't have named them. How did animal foster caregivers do this? It hadn't even been twenty-four sleepless hours, and I was already getting attached to these pups. Judge Beck as well, evidenced by the hundred dollars in toys and treats he'd just bought.

"I know, I know." He glanced back at the pups, who stared at us with big brown eyes and whined. "But they deserve toys. And treats. When they go back, or to another foster, I'll send it all with them. I just thought it would be nice for them to have something to play with or chew. And hopefully stuff like this will keep them occupied during the day so they'll actually sleep at night."

It was a sweet, thoughtful, kind gesture. Things like this made me like him even more.

We drove to the area indicated on Daisy's map, then struggled to get four puppies into their harnesses. The contraptions required several adjustments to fit properly, and the pups were not cooperative at all. Finally, we'd managed to get the harnesses on correctly and snug enough so the pups weren't able to wiggle free or chew on the straps. Then we attached the leashes. I grabbed the stack of flyers and the roll of heavy-duty tape to affix them to poles and signs, and off we went.

Or at least, we tried to be off. Judge Beck had been right.

The pups were not leash trained at all, and immediately became tangled around each other. Starsky rolled over on his back and refused to move. I couldn't exactly drag the guy down the sidewalk, so I stooped to pick him up, and Cagney jumped on me, licking the side of my face.

"You need to walk," I told Cagney. I couldn't carry both puppies plus the flyers. It was going to get old real fast just carrying Starsky. The little guy only weighed five or six pounds, but that didn't mean I was up to lugging a five-pound squirming puppy for the day.

Maybe we should have left them in the SUV in their cages, but I felt bad about that. Trapped in cages for hours? In a cold car? What if they tore up Judge Beck's upholstery? What if one chewed something and choked on it and we weren't there to help? No, I'd rather struggle with stubborn Starsky than risk leaving them behind.

Judge Beck took Starsky from my arms as Hutch and Lacey tangled their leashes around his legs. "Now, look here. We are not going to carry you all over this neighborhood. You're a big boy, and you need to walk like the rest of your siblings. Got it, Starsky?"

He put the pup down and shockingly, Starsky did seem to get it. I stared in amazement as the judge untangled himself and led three puppies down the sidewalk in a somewhat orderly fashion. The guy ran the show in his courtroom *and* on the sidewalks. Evidently law enforcement and accused criminals weren't the only beings that respected the man's firm tone of voice.

"You heard what the judge said," I told Cagney. "Let's go."

My phone beeped, and I glanced at the text, hoping that it was Daisy saying they'd found Lady. It was from Daisy, but not with news about the missing dog.

"Daisy wants me to meet her at Prucilla's," I told the judge. "The niece evidently came in to town early this morning, saw Daisy's note on the door, and called her. She wants to talk to us."

I glanced over at Judge Beck with three puppies tangling their leashes around his legs. He had a stack of flyers in one hand, and a roll of packing tape tucked under one arm. My heart lurched at the sight, doing a giddy little happy-dance.

"Does this invitation include me, or are you going to abandon me with four puppies to continue hanging up flyers on my own?"

There was a teasing tone to his voice that made me smile. "Your choice. If you want to keep hanging up flyers, I'll take the puppies. But you're welcome to come along."

He glanced down at the three pups. "Tell you what. I'll go ahead and hang up flyers and meet you when you're done at Prucilla's. You take Cagney and Starsky, since I think he's going to protest any long walk."

"Deal." I took Starsky's leash and knelt down to unwind the puppy from Judge Beck's legs. Then with a wave, I led both pups the two blocks to Prucilla's house.

CHAPTER 8

"Thank you both for coming here." Prucilla Downing's niece, Grace, paced in the kitchen, twisting her hands together. "I still can't believe she's gone. Aunt Pru was like a force of nature. She was so strong, so committed to her dogs and to animal welfare. I keep expecting her to come around the corner."

"We'd only met your aunt yesterday, but she seemed like a wonderful person. I'm so sorry for your loss," Daisy told her.

Grace nodded, then stooped to pick up Starsky. "When I saw your note this morning, I'd just arrived and was still trying to process everything. But now…I know the police will find her killer, but there's something that would have been more important to Aunt Pru, and that's the dogs."

At her words, a shadowy figure materialized in the corner of the room. I'd seen Prucilla's ghost when I'd stood over her body, and again at the police station, but not since then. Seeing the spirit now, I was surprised she hadn't appeared when Daisy had come by my house last night with the puppies.

Maybe the ghost had hung out with Daisy and the five of

the litter she'd been caring for. But watching the insubstantial form slide through the wall dividing the kitchen from the living room where she'd been murdered, I thought maybe the ghost had instead been searching for Lady. The puppies were safe and well-cared for. And as her niece had said, Prucilla probably would prioritize the safety of the animals over attempts to bring her killer to justice. Lady was lost. And I was positive the ghost had spent the night looking for the dog.

I hoped she'd found Lady. And I hoped that Lady, wherever she was, had been comforted by the spirit's presence.

"We're doing all we can to find Lady," I said, wondering if the ghost could somehow assist in this endeavor. "The pups are being taken care of in Daisy's and my homes. We're happy to keep them until you arrange for fosters or for their adoption."

Grace sighed, rubbing her face in Starsky's fur before putting him down. "That's the problem. I need to go back to work tomorrow. Mom and I are going to take a few days off, but there's a lot we need to deal with in trying to settle Aunt Pru's things. The other dogs are with foster homes, and I've got time over the next few months to work with those people and sort through applications for their foster dogs' adoption, but these puppies need homes now."

"They do," I agreed. At eight to nine weeks, the pups were ready to adopt out.

"Finding Lady and getting good, forever homes for the puppies would have been important to Aunt Pru. I know you're both helping to find Lady, and offered to temporarily care for the puppies, but would you be able to go through applications and help me find good homes for them?" Grace asked. "I'd be willing to pay you for your time. I just need help, and I don't want these puppies to wait months for their families."

"You absolutely don't need to pay me," Daisy told her. "I'm happy to help."

"Me too." I smiled at Grace. "We'll find good homes for the puppies, and we won't rest until we've found Lady."

"Just let us know what sort of criteria we should use in evaluating adoption candidates," Daisy said. "Did Prucilla have a waiting list for the puppies? Is there a specific form she would have wanted us to use?"

"Aunt Pru left her planner on the kitchen table." Grace picked it up and handed it to me. "The police made a copy of it, but didn't take the original. She might have some notes in there about potential adopters for the puppies. She liked both of you ladies. She was going to approve Daisy to adopt Lady even before the application was filled out. Aunt Pru was very picky about who got her dogs, and she was a good judge of character. She trusted you both, and that means I can trust you both as well. I know you'll find good homes for the puppies. And I know you'll find Lady."

"I'll be sure to return it when we're done," I promised the woman, handing her a business card with my contact information.

She took the card, then gave us her phone number and e-mail address as well.

"I'll forward any website applications on the puppies to you," Grace said. "Once I figure out what the password is." She grimaced. "Aunt Pru wrote everything down. I know she probably has a sheet of paper or a book somewhere in her desk or in a bedside table with all her passwords in it. And I'll be in touch if I hear anything about Lady, or if anyone inquires directly about one of the puppies."

"Thanks." I glanced toward the closed door, thinking about the ghost that had slipped through the wall into the living room. "Do you mind if I take a look at Lady's cage as well as those French doors to the backyard? It might give me some ideas on how Lady got out, or if someone might have taken her."

Grace's eyes blinked wide. "Taken her? I hadn't even thought of that. Do you suppose that's why Aunt Pru was killed? Someone wanted to adopt Lady and was angry that she'd been promised to Daisy? Or maybe it was Lady's original owner who wanted her back?"

I held up both hands. "I honestly don't know at this point. It's probably more likely that Lady popped the cage door open, and ran out when your aunt's killer left."

She ran a hand through her hair. "Okay. Sorry, I'm just a little paranoid. Do you mind going in there alone? I haven't been able to. I just don't want to see the mess right now. Eventually I'll need to clean it up, but not now. I can't now."

Daisy put her hand on the woman's shoulder. "There are places you can hire to clean up the room, you know. That way you don't have to do it. If it had been my aunt, I don't think I could face that room either."

I left the two of them in the kitchen, opened the living room door just wide enough to slip through, closing it behind me. When I turned around, I knew right away that Grace shouldn't come in here. The room was almost the same as it had been when Daisy and I had discovered Grace on the floor. Blood stained the taupe and tan carpet. The trophy that I'd assumed had been the murder weapon had been removed, but the others were in a pile on the floor, powder from the fingerprint kits still on them. Prucilla's ghost hovered over the trophies, then moved over to the fireplace mantel where they'd all once been displayed.

Feeling bad that the symbols of her achievement were in a heap on the floor, I went to the pile and picked the broken trophies and plaques up. There was nothing I could do to put them back together again without glue, but at least I could return them to where they'd once been. Sorting through the broken bits, I tried to place them back on the mantel according to my memory.

One was missing—and it wasn't the one the police had taken either. Looking at the awards once more, I closed my eyes and tried to recall which one had been on the left end, right next to the cup-shaped best-in-breed award. Was it the best of owner-bred? Opening my eyes again, I scanned everything and realized that was the one that was missing. I probably wouldn't have noticed except the trophy had caught my eye. I'd been curious that a woman so passionate about rescue dogs had once bred and shown her own, so I'd paid special attention to that award, and remembered it enough to notice it was now gone.

Maybe the police had taken that one too? I pulled out my own notepad and jotted down a quick reminder to check with Miles in the morning.

Looking up, I saw the ghost glide across the floor to hover over Lady's cage.

"We'll find her," I whispered. "Daisy won't give up until she's found, and neither will I."

In response, the door to the cage swung lightly. Prucilla had drawn my attention to the awards, and now the cage. I did believe the ghost was worried about the missing dog, but did she want me to do more than find Lady and take care of the puppies? Were the missing award and the cage clues to where Lady might have gone, or were they clues to who killed Prucilla Downing? Or maybe both.

"Do you want me to discover who murdered you as well as find Lady?" I asked the ghost. "Did the killer take her? Is the killer connected to her in some way?"

Again, the door swung back and forth, this time with a bit more force than before. I went over and knelt down to examine the door and the closures. It was a wire cage, but sturdy. All the welds seemed to be in place, although some of the wires on the door were bowed slightly outward, as if the former occupant had pressed against it in an attempt to pop the catch. There were two latches—one positioned on the top and one on the bottom third of the door. Both used a bolt that slid through metal rings to hold the door closed. It seemed sturdy, but I closed and locked the door and yanked on it, just to make sure. The door held. Yanking with more force, the cage jerked forward, the momentum nearly knocking me backward. Still, the door held. So either the door hadn't been latched properly, or someone had intentionally let Lady out of the cage. Judging from how careful Prucilla had been with her animals, I was betting on the latter.

"The killer attacks Prucilla," I mused. "Lady is probably barking at the commotion. The puppies are probably barking and might even be loose at this point." I frowned. "No, I think the puppies got let loose right before we came in, since they were running out from the living room when we entered the house."

Stepping around the stain on the rug, I tried to envision the scene in my head. "The attacker fights with Prucilla and hits her with a trophy. Lady is barking. The puppies are barking. Then the attacker breaks the other trophies, goes to find a fur coat to slice—or maybe cuts up one he or she brought with her? He...hears us at the door? So he goes to the other room and lets the puppies loose for a distraction in case we come in. Then he goes through the living room, sets Lady free for an additional distraction, and runs out the back door."

I walked over to the back door, the ghost hovering beside me. "Did the killer take Lady with him? Was Lady the reason he was here in the first place?"

The ghost didn't respond, so I tried to dredge up what little I knew about dogs from my friends who had them, as well as my childhood experiences. Kat's dog would probably attack anyone who'd done her harm. Had Lady done the same? She'd only been here less than a day, so it was hard to believe the dog would have considered Prucilla to be her human, but some dogs were just protective. And I could imagine a dog who'd been in an abusive situation might be frightened and lash out at anyone who was acting in a violent manner.

Lady might have bit the murderer, or torn his clothes, I jotted down in my notebook.

There was powder and spray on the door knob and on the door jamb, so the police had dusted for prints, and probably looked for blood. Even if they'd already considered that the attacker might have been injured and bleeding, I'd ask Miles.

"I'm guessing Lady ran out the door after the murderer, either trying to escape or trying to fight the intruder," I mused.

The ghost came closer and I shivered as the icy, shadowy form touched my arm. Then it moved through the closed door and out into the backyard. I opened the door and followed the ghost into the backyard, thinking through what would have happened next.

Prucilla's yard consisted of a flagstone patio that ran the width of the house and a grassy area. A large oak tree had a concrete bench underneath it, and some turned up ground with low fencing to the right looked as if was for annuals, or perhaps vegetables. The whole thing was kept private from the neighboring yards by a high stockade fence that had a gate to the side of the garage and another at the back of the property. The ghost floated toward the back gate, and as I walked over to it, I noticed it wasn't latched. I also noticed residue on the handle and gate from where the police had dusted for prints. It was good to see they'd been thorough.

Swinging the gate open, I poked my head out and saw an alley ran along behind the houses. Past that was an open field that looked to encompass about thirty or forty acres. A house, barn, and grain silo stood off in the distance. A farm. I was sure Daisy had checked with them to see if they'd possibly seen Lady, but I made a mental note to ask her.

As for the intruder, it would have been easy for them to follow the alleyway and duck back around to wherever they'd parked their car. It was quiet and somewhat isolated back here. The stockade fence would hide anyone from the view of the house. Stepping out into the alleyway, I noticed that quite a few houses had similar fences. A person could walk—or run—down this alley and might not be seen.

"Where is Lady?" I asked the ghost. It had led me here, either to show me where the dog had run, or where the killer had run, or possibly both.

In response the ghost headed down the alley, then veered off through the field before vanishing. I followed to the point where the spirit had disappeared but didn't see any clues. The ground was frozen and lumpy without any sign of paw prints or human footprints. I glanced at the farm in the distance, thinking that if Lady had headed this way, she might have sought shelter there. I'd definitely ask Daisy about talking to the residents and seeing if they'd seen a dog sometime last night or this morning.

Making my way back through the field, I latched the backyard gate and went inside. Catching sight of the shredded fur coat, I picked up what looked like it had once been part of a sleeve. I took it with me out into the kitchen where Grace and Daisy were chatting.

"How badly are the trophies broken?" Grace asked me. "Aunt Pru was so proud of those. I'm hoping I can glue them back together."

"I think you should be able to do that," I assured her.

79

"I'm glad," she sighed. "She loved showing and breeding. Mom said that she thought Aunt Pru might be getting back into it again. It was such a big part of her life."

"Getting back into it again?" I asked. "She was thinking about breeding and showing once more?"

Grace shrugged. "Mom mentioned it to me a few weeks ago. She said Aunt Pru was asking her some questions about breeders in the area and their litters, so that's what she assumed. I don't see how Aunt Pru would have had time with her rescue, but who knows."

I thought of Olive and how she was getting back into showing after so many years. Maybe Prucilla had missed the hobby. Who knew, indeed.

"I wanted to ask you: did Prucilla have any fur coats?" I showed Grace the piece I'd picked up. "Do you remember if she had one like this?"

Grace shook her head. "I've never seen her wear one. Aunt Pru wasn't exactly the fur coat type. I'm not saying she didn't have one in a closet somewhere that she might have inherited from her mom or grandmother, but I doubt it. I'll ask mom. She'd know."

I frowned, thinking that if I'd inherited a fur and never wore it, it would probably be in a zippered cover up in a guest room somewhere. It would have been strange for Prucilla's killer to have known about it and its location, and I doubted they would have had opportunity to run upstairs, find it, and shred it in the time between the murder and us arriving.

"Do you mind if I keep this?" I asked. "You can let the police know I have it if they want it for any reason."

"Oh sure. Take all the pieces if you want. I'm not going to do anything but throw it away." She bent down and dug in the cabinet under the sink, coming up with a plastic grocery store bag.

I put the fur piece in the bag and thanked her. "I know you probably talked to the police about this already, but do you know of anyone who might have wanted to harm your aunt? Anyone she mentioned might have been threatening her?"

Grace shook her head. "Not really. I hadn't spoken to her in a few weeks. She and mom were fairly close, so I told the police they should really talk to her. Mom is out of state this week at a show. She packed up as soon as she heard the news, but with the all the equipment and dogs and the drive, she won't be back until tomorrow morning at the earliest."

"Were there any adopters who were mad at her for not letting them have one of the dogs?" Daisy suggested. "Or maybe the owners of that puppy mill she helped shut down?"

Grace frowned in thought. "Probably both. Aunt Pru was very particular about who got her dogs. I'm sure there were quite a few upset people who she refused, but I can't imagine anyone being angry enough over that to kill her. Maybe the puppy mill guy, but there were probably other people who weren't fans of my aunt, too. Even back in her dog show days, she used to get in arguments with people. If she didn't like how someone was treating their dogs, or felt someone had unethical breeding practices, she wasn't shy about speaking up. But I don't know of anyone threatening her, or being so mad at her that they'd resort to murder."

"But someone did," Daisy commented. "Someone was angry enough at your aunt that they came here, killed her, then trashed her trophies and left a destroyed fur coat behind."

"And it looks like she may have let them in," I added. "So it was someone she either knew and trusted, or didn't know, but they had a good reason to be here. Like they were thinking of adopting one of her dogs. There wasn't any sign of forced entry or any signs of struggle anywhere in the house, except for the living room. That makes me think this was personal, and not just some robbery gone wrong."

Grace looked over to the door to the living room. Her hands shook as she placed them on the counter. I immediately felt horrible for upsetting her like this. Her aunt had just been murdered, for Pete's sake, and here I was casually discussing the crime like an unfeeling monster.

"I'm so sorry." I reached out to touch her arm. "I shouldn't have said that. I want your aunt's killer to be brought to justice, but my words were horribly insensitive."

She took a deep breath. "It's okay. I just…I keep forgetting she's gone. It doesn't feel real, and when you said those things, suddenly it became real."

"I'm so sorry," I repeated. "We'll leave so you can do what you need to do here for your aunt. Daisy and I will work on finding Lady and getting good homes for the puppies, and the police will take care of investigating the murder. If you need anything at all, just let Daisy or me know, okay?"

She nodded, tears welling up in her eyes. Daisy and I went to the door, once more offering condolences as we left. We were down the sidewalk before I spoke.

"I feel like a total jerk," I confessed.

"Me too." Daisy sighed. "That poor woman—poor Grace as well as her aunt."

"But we have an official job, or jobs," I told her. "Find Lady. Get the puppies good homes. Did you go to the farm that backs up to Prucilla's and the other houses on her street? I'm thinking Lady might have run that way."

Daisy looked over at me. "I did. There was a bit of a commotion out among the chickens last night, and they think they saw something a little bigger than a fox running away when they went to investigate. I gave them a flyer, and they said they'd put out some food and some deer cameras they use for hunting season, and hopefully they'll spot her."

"And the dog-finding tracking dog?" I asked.

"I'm meeting him at two this afternoon after we hang up flyers and canvass the neighborhood," Daisy said. "Fingers crossed that his dog leads us to Lady, and that she's alive and well."

"Fingers crossed," I repeated. And then I did, indeed, cross my fingers.

CHAPTER 9

I caught up with Judge Beck to hang flyers and question residents while Daisy went to do her section of the neighborhood. Two things became clear as the judge and I worked. One, everyone wanted to talk to you when you had puppies. Two, this neighborhood was just as nosy as mine.

"That woman was in tight with the Free the Fur group," one middle-aged man with a buzz-cut and a neatly trimmed beard told us. "I send them money every year. It's not just the puppy mills and the animal testing in laboratories, you know. Conditions at feed lots are horrible. The way we treat the animals we butcher for meat is cruel. Wanting a cheap burger is no excuse for what those animals go through."

The judge and I exchanged a quick glance. Suddenly I was questioning the contents of my refrigerator and wondering if the local butcher had more ethical practices than the places who sold meat to the grocery stores.

"Tommy Frys is the man." The guy held up a fist as if in solidarity. "I don't think that lady was all that involved in the farm animal or laboratory testing side of things, but she was like a badger when it came to the mistreatment of dogs. I know she and Tommy didn't agree about breeding and dogs shows though. He thinks all that should be outlawed, and I agree. But I don't blame that rescue woman for her views. She helped a lot of dogs when no one else would. She paid for expensive medical surgeries and care when the shelters would'a put a dog down. She helped when puppy mill out near Washdale was shut down. Woman was a saint, even if she did have some wrong views about pedigree dog breeders and stuff."

"Tommy Frys is the person who heads up Free the Fur?" I asked.

The man nodded, then bent down to scratch Hutch behind his ear. "Yeah. Guy's a saint as well. The two of them didn't always see eye-to-eye, but he's gonna be upset about that rescue woman getting whacked. Guess you take that risk when you're a crusader for justice and speaking up for those who can't advocate for themselves, you know?"

"The killer will be caught and prosecuted," Judge Beck told him. "The detective on the case is one of the best in the county."

The man stood. "Yeah. But no jail time will make up for losing all the good that woman would have done had she lived. Who's gonna run her rescue? Who's gonna step up and help those dogs that need help? Who's gonna risk themselves to save dogs from a puppy mill?"

He was right. But hopefully someone would step up and fill in the gap Prucilla's death had left.

"I might be interested in one of these puppies," the man told me. "To honor that rescue woman, you know. My old boy Mack died last year and I haven't had the heart to adopt another dog, but maybe it's time."

I dug around in my purse and handed him a notepad and a pen. "Just put your name, e-mail address, and number down here. I don't have any forms yet, but I'll get something together and send you one. There are nine puppies, and we're taking applications for their adoption."

He wrote down his information and handed the pad and pen back to me. "Good luck finding that missing dog. I'll keep an eye out for her."

I thanked him and the judge and I continued on. As we hung flyers, other people stopped by to gush about how Prucilla had helped shut down the puppy mill. Everyone expressed admiration of her work and her devotion to homeless and abused dogs.

"Not one person we spoke to so far had any problem with Prucilla," Judge Beck commented. "It seems she was loved and admired in the neighborhood."

"I wish someone had information about Lady though." I was torn. As much as my curiosity and nosiness were sparked by the mystery of who had killed Prucilla, my focus needed to be on finding Lady. The longer she was gone, the more chance there was that she'd travel miles away, or get hit by a car, or shot by some farmer, or starve, or freeze. Worry for the dog needed to take priority over my interest in the murder.

After a few more blocks, the judge and I started to work opposite sides of the street so we could make better time. Everyone I spoke to vowed to keep their eyes open for Lady, but none had seen her, or any loose dog, in the neighborhood. Several people had inquired about the puppies, asking if they were mine and making a huge fuss over how cute they were. I took down names and contact information, realizing that I had more than nine people interested in the pups so far.

Would Prucilla's niece or sister take over the rescue, I wondered. Was Grace legally able to give us the authority to adopt the puppies out? Although I hated the thought that these little guys might be in limbo until the legalities of their ownership were straightened out, I was happy that this meant they might be staying with us for a few weeks, or even a month.

Although, I was pretty sure another sleepless night might put the damper on that happiness.

"Is your dog missing?"

I turned around at the voice and saw a woman in her mid-twenties approaching. She pulled a set of earbuds out as she slowed from a jog.

"It's a rescue dog. She escaped when the owner was attacked in her home yesterday," I told her. "Have you seen her around anywhere? The dog I mean."

The woman studied the flyer I'd just taped to the pole of a street sign. "No, but I'll keep my eyes open. Was it one of the dogs from Second Chance? That woman a few blocks down with the rescue?"

"Yes." I switched gears from dog-searcher to private investigator. "Did you know Prucilla Downing?"

The woman started to jog in place. "Not really. I'd see her now and then, but I can't say I really knew her. I read about her working to shut down that puppy mill, though. That makes her a hero in my books."

"Did anyone around the neighborhood have any problems with her? Someone who maybe didn't like all the rescue dogs in and out of her home? Or didn't like people coming and going to apply to adopt the dogs? Or maybe someone who just didn't like how she cut her lawn or the color of her siding?"

The woman tilted her head. "We're not one of those

neighborhoods with a bunch of HOA snobs, and I never heard anyone complain about the rescue dogs. We all thought she was doing a good thing. Wasn't like she had fifty dogs in her house or anything. I think they all went to foster homes after she had them for a week or two."

From what everyone had said, it didn't seem likely that a neighbor had attacked Prucilla. I thanked the woman. She went to jog off, but stopped after a few yards and came back.

"You know, I *did* hear she'd visited some woman in Lakepoint who was breeding Golden Retrievers last week. Maybe that was another puppy mill? Maybe there were unsanitary conditions or something? Or a zoning violation? Oh, and Melissa Burns, who lives next door, said Prucilla and some guy had it out in front of her house on Friday around four o'clock. Guy was a potential adopter or something, and I guess Prucilla had told him no."

I juggled the flyers, the tape, and the leashes with Starsky and Cagney trying to drag me down the street and managed to jot the information on the notepad. Melissa Burns. I'd need to talk to her. Or the police would. I hated to think getting turned down for a dog adoption would cause someone to murder another, but I'd seen more disturbing things than that in my years of journalism and my last year as a private investigator. As for the Golden Retriever woman, I'd definitely check that one out, too.

"Thanks," I called after the woman as she jogged away.

After two additional blocks I'd found three people who thought they'd seen a loose dog the prior night, but weren't positive if it was Lady or not. Actually, none of them were positive it was even a dog or not. One thought it might have been a fox, and the other wasn't sure if what he'd seen was a deer or a dog. I jotted down where they thought they'd seen the dog and approximately what time along with their contact information and kept going. By this point, poor little Cagney and Starsky were exhausted, and I'd started carrying the pups half tucked inside my parka. Judge Beck had turned down one of the side streets several blocks back, and I wondered if he was having to carry Hutch and Lacey as well.

I was almost finished with my circuit by lunchtime and I could see Judge Beck ahead of me, coming down the block. Sure enough, he had two puppies in his arms—both of which he needed to set down each time he hung up a flyer. I hurried up a bit and stuffed the remaining flyers in one of my coat pockets.

"Did you find anyone who has seen Lady?" I asked him, tucking my scarf around the puppies I was carrying and thinking we should have gotten them little sweaters. They would be so adorable in little sweaters. I wished I was good enough at knitting to make them each one, but I hadn't been adventurous enough to make more than those Christmas scarves for my friends.

"A few people thought they might have seen an animal last night, but no one was positive whether it was a dog or not." Judge Beck adjusted the two puppies he was carrying so they were cradled one in each arm.

"Same here," I told him. "I *did* get a few leads on murder suspects, though. Seems a neighbor saw Prucilla having an argument with a potential adopter Friday evening, and I heard she went to visit a woman in Lakepoint who breeds Golden Retrievers."

We turned to head back toward the SUV. Thankfully, we'd walked in a bit of a loop, so it wasn't more than a few blocks from us.

"I think if a potential adopter was going to attack Prucilla, he would have done it Friday when they were actually having the argument," I mused.

"Not necessarily," Judge Beck replied. "Some people get more upset with time, especially if the adopter had a friend or family member harping on the injustice and stoking their anger."

I thought about that for a second. "True. Or maybe the killer was this Golden Retriever lady. Or the guy who ran the puppy mill."

"If it's the puppy mill guy, he's a fool," the judge commented. "That was all over the papers. He's got to know he'd be at the top of the suspect list."

"Maybe he doesn't care," I said. "You did say some people get more upset with time. He's lost everything. Maybe he wanted Prucilla to lose everything as well."

We turned the corner, and I saw the SUV parked down the next block—which was a good thing. These puppies were getting heavy.

"Do you think the killer took Lady?" I wondered. "Maybe the murderer is Lady's former owner. Prucilla said Lady came from a hoarding situation. Maybe the owner was upset over losing her animals, came to get Lady back, and got into a fight with Prucilla."

"It's a possibility. I've seen assault cases, and even murder cases, over pets before." The judge sighed. "Judge Sanchez always said the biggest sticking point in his divorce cases is who gets the dog. It made me glad that was one less thing Heather and I had to fight over."

"How is that going? Your divorce, I mean?" The moment I'd said it, I wished I could take the words back. It was none of my business. I shouldn't be prying into his and Heather's legal matters.

He stopped and turned to face me. "I was going to tell you last night, but things got a little busy with the puppies and all. The one-year anniversary for Heather's and my separation was last month, while we were on vacation. We submitted the final paperwork as soon as I got back, and I just got the decree Friday. I am officially a divorced man."

Relief flooded through me. Whatever was between us would progress a lot easier now that he was a no longer legally married. I knew that sort of thing mattered to Judge Beck, and it mattered to me as well. His marriage had been over when he'd become my tenant, but having it official somehow made this tentative romance feel more honest... and more right.

"Are you...how do you feel about that?" I might be giddy with excitement, but he and Heather had been married for almost two decades. There had to be some sadness mixed in with the sense of closure.

He smiled. "Good, actually. I've mourned the loss of my marriage, and now I think I'm in a place where I just see it as a part of my past. There were lots of happy memories, and some not so happy ones. I'm ready to make new memories, to make a new future."

I wanted to loop my arm in his, to take his hand in mine. If only the both of us didn't have our arms full of puppies.

"I'm happy for you. And Heather. And the kids." From what I could see, Madison and Henry had adjusted to their parents' separation and pending divorce, and seemed to be okay.

My phone beeped, and I juggled puppies to pull it out of my coat pocket. I sucked in a breath when I saw the text was from Daisy. Careful not to drop either Cagney or Starsky, I opened the message and squealed.

"She found her! Lady's been found! The farm behind Prucilla's house? They've got her locked in their barn. Daisy's heading over now to see if she can get her out."

Judge Beck reached out and took Starsky from me. "Then I'll drop you off at the farm so you can help Daisy. I'll take these guys home and get them fed and taken care of."

I smiled up at him. "Thank you. Thank you for everything."

He returned my smile. "Absolutely. Now come on. You've got a runaway rescue dog to save, and I've got four sleepy, hungry puppies to take care of."

CHAPTER 10

The driveway up to the farm was gravel and full of potholes. Cattle eyed us from the fence line, their pasture of stubbled brown grass dotted with stacks of hay. Two cars and three trucks were parked by the barn, with half a dozen people clustered around the huge door. One man lugged a wire crate up from a shed, and another pulled some kind of netting off the back of one of the trucks. Daisy stood by the barn door, her hand on the weathered gray wood.

Judge Beck pulled to a stop beside the other vehicles, then glanced in the back at the puppies who'd slept through all the bouncing. "Do you need me to assist? These guys look like they're fine in the car. I can leave it running with the heat on and help corral Lady."

I felt bad enough about making him hang up signs and question neighbors all morning. Add to that the fact that I'd saddled him with four puppies, and I hated to ask him to do anything else.

"It looks like these people have things in hand." I gestured to the net and the cage, wondering if all this was necessary. Lady wasn't a rabid badger, she was a dog. Yes, she'd been neglected for a good bit of her life, but would we really need to net her and stuff her in a cage?

"Are they trapping a bear or catching a runaway dog," Judge Beck echoed my thoughts. "I'd imagine all this would scare her worse than if someone just went in with a plate of roast beef and bacon."

My stomach growled. "I'd let someone put a leash on *me* for roast beef and bacon."

Did that sound naughty? It might have sounded naughty.

"Me too," he replied. "Do you want me to order pizza delivery here? If you don't think this will take more than an hour, I can have some lunch ready at home."

I thought about that for a second. "Thanks, but no. Knowing Daisy, she's going to want to take this slow and not risk scaring Lady. I'll text you when we're heading home. It won't kill me to skip lunch, and I've got chicken enchiladas made up and in the fridge for dinner tonight."

"Do you need me to throw them in the oven?" he asked.

This felt so domestic. I loved it.

"If I'm going to be later than five, I'd love for you to get it started." I glanced back at the group by the barn. "I'm hoping it won't take that long. Daisy is really good at getting surly and frightened teens to trust her. I'm hoping that makes her a runaway-dog whisperer as well."

I got out of the SUV, zipping my coat up against the cold wind coming across the empty fields. Judge Beck turned his vehicle around and headed back down the drive as I walked over to Daisy and the crowd.

Daisy introduced me to the farmer and his family, then put her hand back on the barn door and grinned. "Russ said he pulled the tractor in to get a bale of hay about half an hour ago and saw her curled up in the pile of bedding in the back of the barn. She didn't seem spooked, but he closed the doors and locked her in before calling me."

"Just in case she got it in her head to run off," Russ added.

"I'm hoping I can convince her to come to me so I can put a slip leash on her." Daisy glanced over at the net. "If not, we may need to try a few other things."

"Hopefully those other things include bits of roast beef and bacon," I said. "I don't know much about dogs, but I think food bribes might work better than throwing a net over her."

"We've got hotdogs and some liver snacks," Russ spoke up. "But scared dogs don't always come for treats."

Daisy held up a plastic bag full of the cut-up bits of meat. "Are you ready? I'm going to put down some treats, get as close to her as I can, then sit and hope for the best. I want you to stay inside the door, so she doesn't try to run out. Russ is going to put the cage by the door and have the net ready. If I can't get her to come to me, we'll need to try to herd her into the cage. If that doesn't work, we've got the net."

I hoped it didn't come to that.

With a long exhale, Daisy pushed the barn door open just wide enough for the two of us to squeeze through. The guys put the cage at the opening, then backed out of view. My eyes adjusted to the dark of the barn, and my nose tickled with the smell of hay and wood shavings. To the right, huge round bales of hay were stacked three-high in rows. To the left, piles of shavings and mulch filled that section of the barn. I stood near the barn door while my friend eased forward, searching for any sign of where Lady might be.

A low growl sounded from the pile of shavings and I saw a hunched shape cower farther down, slowly moving backward.

Daisy sat. I did the same, trying to look everywhere but at the dog while keeping her in my peripheral vision. Daisy opened the bag of treats, spreading the top of the bag wide so the smell could waft out and reach the dog. Lady had to have been hungry. She'd missed her dinner last night, and probably hadn't had anything to eat all day in this barn.

Daisy pulled a few pieces of meat from the bag, rolling them in her fingers before tossing them far enough away from her that Lady would need to move closer to get them, but not so close that it would feel as if she were lobbing something directly at the dog.

Lady's nose twitched. She scooted a few feet forward on her belly, then stopped, stretching her neck as if she were trying to reach the food that was still a good four feet away.

Daisy waited, playing with the food in the bag as she sat absolutely quiet, never once looking directly at Lady or moving from where she sat. I tried to remain still. After half an hour, Lady had moved close enough to eat the first treats Daisy had thrown and was eyeing the second batch. Meanwhile, I was pretty sure my left leg had fallen asleep.

Daisy tossed some more treats, these ones closer to her.

The dog seemed to like the bits of hotdog and liver. She ate those closest to her, then began sniffing the ground for more. When the dog realized there was another batch closer to Daisy, she didn't hesitate to scoot on her belly for the second set of treats. After she finished those, she stood, sniffing around and slowly making her way to the third set.

Daisy had infinite patience, remaining calm as Lady countered every few steps forward with a few steps back. After an hour in the barn, she was only a few feet from my friend, eyeing the bag that was now only half full of treats. Then suddenly the dog closed the distance, sitting right next to my friend and shoving her head right into the bag to devour the snacks. Daisy stroked her gently, remaining quiet and not making any sudden moves as Lady scarfed down the treats. Lady didn't even flinch when Daisy looped the leash around her neck. Even after she'd gotten the leash on the dog, Daisy still sat, letting the dog eat as she petted her and whispered soft words of affection.

My eyes stung with tears at the sight of the two of them together. I may have questioned Daisy's decision to adopt the dog she'd seen for all of five minutes, the dog who'd just been rescued from a hoarding situation and might not be at all ready for a forever home, but seeing them both like this made me realize that Daisy knew what she was doing. She knew her heart. And just as she knew what the teenagers she worked with needed, she knew what Lady needed as well.

When the bag was empty, Daisy eased it away and scratched Lady behind the ears. "It's all gone, girl, but I've got other good stuff at the house. We'll get you a bath and shave these matts out of your coat, then you can have a decent dinner and some water. Some of the puppies are there for company. Tomorrow you and the puppies can all go into work with me. I think you'll like it there. You can hang out in a crate in my office where it's nice and quiet, or come meet everyone. I know all the kids I work with will like you. And the puppies will be glad to see you."

I watched her pet the dog and talk to it, not moving until she felt Daisy was ready. Then I saw her stand. Standing wasn't easy for me after over an hour of sitting on the cold, hard ground while trying to be quiet and still, but I managed. With a quick wave of my hand, Russ and his boys had moved the cage out of the way and opened the door wide enough for us to exit. They stood by the side, net ready just in case the dog changed her mind and tried to bolt.

But Lady had made her decision, and she stuck with it. She waltzed out on the leash beside Daisy as if she were competing at Westminster instead of exiting a barn with shavings and hay stuck to her matted and dirty fur. I didn't know the dog's background, but I hadn't expected this at all. Daisy led her to the car, opened the back seat, and I watched as the dog hopped right on in. The puppies were in a frenzy of excitement to see their friend. Lady nosed the cages, her tail wagging like crazy as Daisy put the dog's harness on and secured the apparatus to the seatbelt.

I felt my whole body sag in relief once she closed the car door. We'd done it. We'd found Lady less than twenty-four hours after she'd gone missing. We'd found her safe and unhurt. And Daisy had her in the car, ready to go to her new home. A happy ending.

And I got the feeling the shadowy form hovering by Daisy's car felt the same.

We thanked the farmer and his family for their help and climbed into the car. The noise from the back seat was deafening as we pulled down the gravel drive, but the sound made me happy.

"I'll text Grace and let her know we've found Lady and that she's safe and on her way to her new home," I told Daisy.

"Let her know I've got at least four people interested in adopting one of the puppies as well," Daisy said as I texted.

"Send me their contact information," I told her. "I've got about nine interested, and I'm thinking it's best if we consolidate and have one person send out the applications. I wonder if J.T. will let me have Molly's help for an hour or two tomorrow to e-mail everyone and do some reference checks?"

Daisy laughed. "He definitely will. He's very motivated to find these guys their forever homes. The puppies are putting a cramp in our romance."

"Tell me about it," I groused.

"And how is this romance between you and the judge going?" Daisy grinned. "Details, girl. I want details."

"I have no details to share at this time." And I didn't think I'd be sharing *all* of the details with Daisy, even after they happened. "He did invite me to go out for dinner Valentine's Day, though."

"Are you okay with that?" She shot me a quick glance. "I know it was always a big day for you and Eli."

"I explained that to him, and let him know that I wanted to swing by the cemetery beforehand to put some flowers and a card on Eli's grave."

Daisy made an "oof" noise. "How did he take that? I mean, stopping by the cemetery to visit the gravesite of your date's late husband isn't exactly romantic."

It wasn't, and I was grateful that Judge Beck had been so understanding about the whole thing.

"At first he offered to celebrate on a different evening, but I convinced him that everything was okay and that I was excited to be having dinner with him afterward." The activity might put a slight damper on the romance of the evening, but this is who we were. My husband had passed not quite a year ago. He was newly divorced. We each had a past, and our future would depend on us being able to work with and accept the past that each of us carried.

"I expect to hear details the next morning," she warned me as she turned down our street. "Details, Kay."

I grinned. "Am I going to hear the details of your romantic Valentine's Day date with J.T.?"

"Absolutely." She glanced in the rearview at the backseat. "Although I'm not sure how romantic our evening is going to be with five puppies and Lady as chaperones. I'm not going to leave them alone in the house this soon. I guess J.T. will need to cancel our reservations. We'll cook something at my house instead."

Oh no. The puppies. Thankfully, Henry and Madison were with us this week. I didn't think they'd mind watching the little guys for the judge and me. Maybe they could watch

Daisy's crew as well—although I'd want to discuss that with them and the judge before suggesting the idea to Daisy.

Heather's SUV was in the driveway as Daisy pulled in. I eyed it, noting that she'd brought the kids over early. That was a rare happening. I wondered if having their divorce finalized had taken some of the tenseness out of her and the judge's interactions. The last year it had seemed as if each of them were carefully jockeying for position, afraid that one slight misstep would cost them custody. Hopefully that was over and the family would begin to heal and trust that the other had only good motives and intentions.

I went inside and found chaos. The puppies were barking and racing loose in the house. Henry was on all fours, laughing as he chased them down. Madison was trying to appear disinterested, but there was a faint smile on her lips as she knelt down, videoing the madness. No doubt it would all soon appear on SnapChat or TikTok or some other social media platform.

Heather picked Cagney up, running her hands over the puppy's light brown fur. "This is unexpected! When did you and Nate decide to get puppies? And *four*?"

You and Nate. As if we were a couple, and Heather had no problem at all with that. I was sure she probably meant it as in house-owner and tenant, but I registered it differently. It felt good—as if she accepted us as an *us.*

"It's unexpected on our part as well," I told her. "We're fostering them. The rescue…had an emergency. Daisy has five, and we have four—until they're adopted."

"Well, you'll have no problem finding these guys homes." She touched her nose to Cagney's. "No she won't. Because you're so cute, aren't you? You're just adorable."

"Want one? I can print out an application for you."

"Oh no." Heather shoved the puppy into my arms. "Don't

tempt me. I always wanted a dog, but never felt like I had the time to care for one."

I thought about the judge's knee-jerk reaction to seeing Gus. He'd wanted a dog too, and, according to him, Heather had been the one to always answer with a firm no to that. Although I couldn't really blame her. She'd been raising two kids, and even Judge Beck admitted he'd not been home a lot. All the care, training, and upkeep for a dog would have fallen on her already-burdened shoulders.

But now...

"The kids are old enough to help," I said to her. "Are you sure you're not interested?"

"That's definitely something I would need to think long and hard about." She reached out and scratched Cagney's ears.

Just then, the judge poked his head out of the kitchen. "I heated up the oven for the enchiladas and put them in. Heather, thanks for bringing the kids by early. I really needed their help with these puppies."

"No problem," she replied with a wave of her hand. "I'll get out of your hair then. Enjoy your dinner. I'll be by Sunday to pick the kids up."

I saw Heather out, then went into the kitchen to help with dinner. Along with the enchiladas, I'd planned on cooking up some black beans and making fresh guacamole. Judge Beck remained in the kitchen, making the guac, while I put the beans on the stove and started helping him chop avocados.

"I take it the dog recovery was a success?" he asked as he diced onions. "Lady is home safe with Daisy and her half of the puppy crew?"

"Yes." Once more relief washed over me. "Daisy was amazing. She sat there for an hour, luring Lady in with bits of hot dogs and liver. She was so patient."

"And now you only have to find homes for nine puppies," the judge commented.

"We've got over a dozen people that expressed interest," I told him. "We'll see how many are still interested come tomorrow and send them applications. I want to be just as picky as Prucilla would have been, though. So it might be a few weeks before the puppies have all found new homes."

The judge glanced into the hallway where his children were racing around with the puppies and Taco, who'd decided to join in the fun. "Will we be able to survive two weeks of this? Will Taco be able to survive two weeks of this?"

I laughed. "Taco seems to be adjusting just fine. I'm sure the kids will be happy to help us this week. As for next week...well, let's try to be positive and hope at least two or three of the pups will have gone to their forever homes by then."

He smiled over at me. "I honestly don't mind. I do worry that I'm going to start getting attached to them, though."

It was a valid concern, given that he'd spent roughly a hundred dollars on toys and treats this morning. I was worried about getting attached as well. They had their own individual personalities, and I was beginning to fall in love with each of them. It would be hard to let them go, but I knew I couldn't manage four puppies that would turn into four grown dogs. I could barely handle having a cat.

"Oh! I almost forgot! Do you think Madison and Henry could watch the puppies while we go out to dinner on Valentine's? I hate to abandon them with four rowdy puppies without at least asking first."

He glanced into the foyer again. "I can pretty much guarantee that the answer to that will be an excited 'yes.'"

"Do you think they could watch the other five puppies

and Lady so Daisy and J.T. can go out?" I frowned. "I'm worried that might be too much for them."

"They're good kids, and I know they're responsible and sensible. I'd absolutely trust them with four puppies and a cat, but I think that's the limit of what they can handle." Judge Beck grimaced. "I'm sorry, Kay. I know you'd like to help your friend out."

I felt bad that they were going to miss their first Valentine's Day together, but J.T. would need to realize that responsibility always came first with Daisy. It was one of the things that made her such an amazing person and such a valuable friend, but it also meant plans occasionally would get cancelled. I was sure that J.T. would rather have Valentine's Day dinner at Daisy's with a dog and five puppies than alone. I knew my boss loved Daisy, and if her love came with a dog and five foster puppies, then he'd go with it.

"I think the enchiladas and the beans are done," the judge said. "Let me finish the guacamole while you set the table. The kids can put the puppies away, feed Taco, then we'll all sit down and have a nice, quiet dinner."

At that moment, all four puppies began barking and howling. We'd definitely have a nice dinner, but I doubted it would be quiet.

CHAPTER 11

glanced at the clock, thinking that I really should go to bed. Tomorrow was Monday, and I needed to be at work early—and awake even earlier for Daisy's and my yoga. I'd barely slept last night and couldn't afford another night with only a few hours of rest. The puppies were worn out by today's walk and playing with the kids, and for once were actually sleeping. I needed to be in my pajamas and curling up in bed, but instead I was sitting down at the dining room table with my laptop.

Pulling out my pad of paper, I reviewed my notes and jotted down some names.

Tommy Frys and Free the Fur.

Puppy Mill Guy.

Golden Retriever breeder in Lakepoint.

Lady's former owner—hoarder case.

Applicant that Prucilla argued with on Friday.

Chewing on my lip in thought, I made a little "x" next to Tommy Frys name. He and Prucilla might not have seen eye-to-eye on everything, especially her dog-show past, and the broken trophies as well as the slashed coat did seem to point to a killer who had strong views on the treatment of animals. But Free the Fur and Prucilla had worked together in getting the puppy mill shut down. From what my friends and Prucilla's neighbors said, both seemed to be on good terms with each other. It seemed a stretch to think Tommy Frys would want Prucilla dead. The smashed trophies and destroyed fur could have been an attempt to misdirect the investigation, as Judge Beck had suggested. I still wanted to go see Tommy Frys and ask him for information, but I didn't consider him a strong suspect at this point.

Firing up the laptop, I found the contact information for Tommy Frys off the Free the Fur website and sent him a quick e-mail asking if I could meet with him tomorrow afternoon.

Then I searched both newspaper articles and courthouse records about the puppy mill case. The owner of the puppy mill, Choice Breeders LLC, was a man named Rich Reed. According to the newspaper article, animal control had seized sixty-two dogs and twelve puppies, and the police were charging Reed with animal neglect. Reed was counter suing to get his animals back, and was quoted in the paper as saying he was running a breeding business under an agricultural license, and that the conditions at Choice Breeders were in line with those standards. He claimed all the puppies sold to nationwide pet stores had received veterinary exams and appropriate vaccinations, and that the breeding animals were well taken care of.

Eying the pictures that accompanied the article, I felt differently. Cement floor dog runs lined the walls of a dilapidated barn. The dogs inside were almost as matted and dirty as poor Lady had been. Yes, they looked well-fed, and each run had clean water, but there was barely room for the dogs to move around. Dull eyes stared at the camera, and my heart twisted for each and every one of those dogs. These animals were having two litters each year from the moment of their first heat and were dumped at rescues and shelters after they reached the point where they were no longer able to produce puppies. Although I was relieved that Reed didn't just put them down at that point, and was glad the older dogs looked forward to some decent quality of life in their latter years, I still felt sick over the whole thing. Five, seven, or even ten years of life in a small pen, having litter after litter with no one to scratch their ears, rub their belly, tell them they were good dogs. No soft beds to lay on, children to play with, walks with interesting smells. No special treats. The whole thing brought tears to my eyes. I was so grateful that Prucilla and Free the Fur had shut this thing down. Hopefully, one day, no dog would ever have to live like that again.

I wondered what fosters had the sixty-two dogs and twelve puppies? I assumed with a counter suit being filed, the rescues wouldn't be able to adopt them out just yet. At least they were in good homes where they could run and play and experience love for the first time in their lives.

It seemed as if Rich Reed certainly had a motive for wanting Prucilla dead. She'd helped destroy his business. She'd been instrumental in getting all of his dogs removed from his care. But why go after Prucilla and not Tommy Frys and the Free the Fur group who'd actually gotten more press in the case? Why kill Prucilla and not Tommy?

Plus, there was the fact that Reed was fighting the case and trying to get his animals back. Killing Prucilla seemed to be the action of a person with nothing left to lose, and I didn't think Rich Reed had reached the level of anger or despair that he'd throw away every last chance of getting his business back just for a revenge killing.

I glanced at the clock and winced, promising myself that I'd go to bed after just a little more research.

The only Golden Retriever breeder I could find listed in Lakepoint was a woman named Vicky Ellinger who ran a kennel called Victory Lake Goldens. The website had pictures of six different dogs at dog shows, as well as doing scent tracking and obedience. Other pictures showed the dogs being loved on by children and posing with silly birthday hats. They were gorgeous dogs with glossy coats, kind brown eyes, and expressions full of joy.

Victory Lake Goldens did not look like the sort of operation that Prucilla would be going after, but I knew as well as anyone how website pictures could make an organization look to be something they weren't. For all I knew, Victory Lake Goldens was just as horrible as Rich Reed's puppy mill, only packaged up to look happy and family-friendly. Maybe this place was truly terrible and Vicky Ellinger had killed Prucilla before the woman could get her operation shut down. Or maybe Victory Lake wasn't the Golden Retriever breeder that the jogging neighbor was talking about. Maybe there was another breeder in Lakepoint that wasn't coming up on my Google search, and *that* was the one Prucilla had gone to see last week.

I put a question mark next to Victory Lake Goldens and went back to the newspaper to look up the case of Lady's former owner. The article was from two days ago and didn't list the owner's name or address, just that animal control had seized twenty dogs and thirty-five cats from a house in the sixteen-hundred block of Angler Road in Milford. I made a note of the date and vague location, knowing that a call to the courthouse in the morning would get me the rest of the information.

I didn't know how much Prucilla had to do with animal

control coming to the hoarder's house, but she *had* ended up with Lady. I could absolutely see someone being upset and wanting to get their dogs and cats back—and violently attacking anyone who stood in their way. My only experience with hoarders was with my former neighbor across the street. Mr. Peter had become agitated and violent on occasion, but I'd always viewed him as a frustrated, lonely man who had grossly overestimated his ability to repair the mountain of broken appliances in his home. I thought back on my few encounters with Mr. Peter, trying to envision how he would have reacted had someone condemned his property, hauled all of his appliances and junk away. Just the threat of that sort of thing had led him to attack his own nephew.

I didn't even know this Angler Road woman's name, but she was definitely moving up on my suspect list.

Last was the applicant that Prucilla's neighbor had seen her arguing with Friday. I glanced at the planner that Grace had given me and decided not to go down that rabbit hole right now. If I started looking through that, I'd be up all night, and I needed to get *some* sleep in order to function at work tomorrow.

J.T. would have cases for me to research, and I didn't think my boss would let me push that work aside to spend all day sending out puppy-adoption applications and sticking my nose into a case that I was *not* getting paid to investigate. He definitely would want the puppies adopted out sooner rather than later, and I was sure I could talk him into letting Molly work on that for a few hours tomorrow, but the murder…

I'd just need to work faster and smarter and make time for my own investigation. I could meet with Tommy Frys over my lunch hour. And I could always take work home with me. I'd done it before, and now that J.T. wasn't paying me overtime any longer, he allowed me to be far more flex-ible with my schedule.

So, I'd leave the rest of my nosy-lady sleuthing for tomor-row. I was going to go to bed—and hopefully I'd get a decent four or five hours of sleep until the puppies woke me up and demanded my immediate attention.

* * *

I WAS UP AT FIVE, feeding puppies as well as Taco and getting organized for my day. Daisy arrived promptly at six with her entire entourage of four-legged friends and led them around to the backyard. Lady's undernourished state was even more evident now that she'd been washed and had the mats clipped from her fur, but the dog trotted at the end of her leash with a confident, happy step. She was gray and white, looking even more like a terrier with her new 'do. I had no doubt that Daisy would soon have the dog's weight up, and once she filled out, Lady would be even more adorable than she was now.

I poured a cup of coffee to take to Daisy, then unleashed my own hounds. The four bounded down the porch steps to the yard, yipping and excitedly greeting their siblings and Lady.

All this at six in the morning. My neighbors were going to hate me.

"Here." I handed Daisy her coffee, wishing that I'd put some whisky in both our mugs. Although as tired as I was, I needed the caffeine more than the soothing buzz of alcohol.

She chugged the contents of her mug, then set it aside, safely out of reach of puppies and Lady, all of whom were racing around my backyard.

Our opening poses weren't quiet contemplative moments today. As we moved from forward-fold to plank to cobra to downward dog, puppies ran between our legs and arms, occasionally pausing to lick our hands and faces. I started to giggle as Cagney tugged on my T-shirt with her sharp little teeth, then burst into full-on laughter as Lady jumped over Daisy's back, chasing three of the puppies. After a few sun salutations, we gave up and rolled up our mats.

I brought out some toys for the pups as well as a blanket for us and refilled both of our coffee mugs. We sat on a bench, wrapped ourselves in the blanket and drank coffee as Lady played with the puppies.

"So...are Madison and Henry going to puppy sit for the two of you, or will you both be celebrating a home-cooked Valentine's Day meal like J.T. and I?" Daisy asked.

"Judge Beck gave the idea his approval, and both kids were excited about it." I winced, feeling guilty that we were going out while she and J.T. couldn't.

"That's awesome." She sighed. "J.T. is going to kill me. He made dinner reservations months ago."

"Isn't there someone who can puppy sit for you?" I asked. "Suzette and Olive? Someone else? I thought about offering to have Madison and Henry watch the whole bunch, but it's really too much for them."

"Oh definitely. Nine puppies and a new rescue dog? It *is* too much," she was quick to assure me. "I'll find someone. Or I won't." She shrugged "And if we have to celebrate at my house, then I'll just make it up to J.T. later."

I laughed at that. "He adores you. You won't have to work too hard to make it up to him."

"Oh, I don't know." She grinned. "Enough about me. What are you getting the judge for a Valentine's Day present?"

Oh no. I couldn't believe I'd forgotten about that. If I was going to make a card and put it and flowers by Eli's grave, then not having *anything* for Judge Beck would be rude. But what to get him? Eli had been the gift-giver for this holiday in our relationship, not me, so I had no real idea what to get the judge.

"A card? Flowers? No, I can't do that." It would be weird to get the judge the same things I was leaving on the gravesite of my deceased husband. And cards were tricky. A light and funny one might be…well, too light and funny. I didn't want to get all mushy at this early stage of our relationship either.

"Candy?" I threw out there. Although the judge was more of a cookie person. Maybe some fancy cookies? Would I have time to make them with work and puppies and trying to find Prucilla's murderer? I'd have to make something if I decided on a baked-good gift, because store-bought would seem thoughtless after all the baking I'd done this year.

"I'm getting J.T. beef jerky in a heart," Daisy announced.

"A what? Did you say beef jerky? In a *heart*?" I turned to face my friend in astonishment.

"He loves beef jerky, and I found a place that does little sample packets of different flavors and puts it in a heart, like it's candy." Daisy explained.

Should I get something like that for the judge? I'd never seen him eat beef jerky before, and three pounds of dried sirloin seemed like a really strange gift.

"I wish I had time to knit him covers for his golf clubs," I said. "He loves golf, and I could make him a set with his initials embroidered on them."

"What else does he like?" Daisy asked.

"Coffee, but the kids got him that coffee-of-the-month subscription and a mug for his birthday. They always get him quirky pajamas too, but I think we're kind of early in our relationship for me to be buying him that sort of thing, even if I got something silly like with bears and hearts on them."

"You'll think of something." Daisy handed me her empty mug, pushed the blanket off her lap and stood. "I guess I better get all these dogs home and get ready for work. It's going to be absolute chaos bringing a dog and five puppies to work with me today."

It wouldn't be much better for me with four puppies. Hopefully the cold morning romp had tired them enough that they'd be calm and sleep a lot. If not, it was going to be a rough day for all of us.

CHAPTER 12

"*I*'m sorry I'm late," I called out to J.T. as I struggled to get four puppies on leashes through the office door.

"Oh!" Molly jumped up, rushing over to untangle the leashes and help get them inside. "Are these yours? They're adorable."

J.T. was scowling at the puppies. I bit back a smile, knowing that he'd spent a few hours yesterday dealing with the five Daisy was taking care of. Molly might think the little furballs were adorable, but J.T. clearly had a different opinion.

"We're trying to find the puppies good homes," I told him. "Including the ones Daisy has."

His expression brightened at that, and I realized that my boss might be far more supportive of this task than I'd thought.

"The sooner we get applications to these people and check their references and eligibility, the sooner these pups can go to their new homes," I told him.

"Can that be by five o'clock tomorrow?" J.T. scrubbed a hand over his face. "I made Valentine's Day dinner reservations at that new French place in Stallworth two months ago, and Daisy's warning me that I'm either going to have to cancel the reservations or figure out how to convince a swanky restaurant to allow five puppies as well as Lady into the dining area."

"You know there are companies where you can hire someone to dog-sit." Molly picked up Starsky and snuggled him against her chest. "A smart boyfriend would make one phone call, shell out some cash, and have a trustworthy person watch the dogs while he and Daisy are out having a carefree evening."

"There are companies that do that?" I asked as J.T. immediately got out his phone and began typing. Babysitting had been my main gig as a teenager. I could absolutely see enterprising teens being paid to watch pets while their owners went out, but a company? A company that specialized in dog-sitting?

"Yes, there are companies that do that." She grinned. "They've got pet sitters and even pet walkers that come by your house while you're at work and take Fido for an exercise stroll. Some of them even have doggie day-care places where people drop their pets off so they don't have to spend the day in a cage while their owners are at work."

"Holy cow. Look at these rates," J.T. grumbled. "What a racket. How can they charge that just to sit in a house for an evening and make sure none of the dogs die or eat the curtains? Good grief. There's an added fee for multiple dogs and an added fee for dogs under six months. This is going to cost more than the dinner."

"Romance isn't for the faint of heart or the light of wallet," I teased. "Maybe you know a reputable young woman who likes puppies and might be interested in making a little extra money?" I nodded at Molly. "Someone, perhaps, sitting right here in this office?"

"I'll pay you five bucks an hour to pet sit," J.T. hurriedly offered her, as if he feared I might beat him to the punch.

"Isn't the going rate for babysitting ten an hour?" I bit back a smile at the look of horror on his face. "Yes, I think the Peterson's mentioned that's what they've been paying their sitter."

"That's for kids," he argued. "This is a dog. It's a lot easier to watch a dog than to watch children. Seven an hour and I'll throw in a pizza."

"There's one dog and *five* puppies," I said before Molly could reply. "You puppy sat yesterday. Tell me how much easier it is to watch one or two children as opposed to five not-housebroken puppies."

I swear he paled when I mentioned "not housebroken." Clearly he hadn't had Judge Beck's foresight to get the pee pads from the pet store.

"Eight an hour," he counter offered. "Pizza and soda. And I'll let you help Kay find the puppies new homes for no more than three hours each day until they're gone...I mean, adopted."

Molly grinned. "Can I bring my brother, Hunter? He'd be thrilled to spend the evening with a dog and a bunch of puppies."

"Then you should really order two pizzas," I told J.T., trying to keep from laughing at the scowl he shot me.

"Okay, two pizzas. But I'm not paying your brother. Just you. And it's eight dollars an hour starting from when you get to Daisy's house and ending when we get back home. I'm not paying for travel time."

J.T. was so cheap. But I knew that once he and Daisy were

out for the evening, her company would be a whole lot more valuable than the eight dollars an hour he was paying Molly. Plus, I was pretty sure Daisy would insist on him giving the girl and her brother a tip once they got back.

J.T. would do it because he was in love. People in love did silly things. Like spend a hundred dollars at the pet store on a bunch of puppies that had been foisted on you. Like offer to take care of those same puppies when you probably had other plans for the day. Like call your ex-wife and ask her to bring the kids over early to help take care of those puppies.

Friends did that too. Friends. I wasn't in a position to assign any emotional motives to Judge Beck beyond friendship. I wasn't quite ready to entertain the thought of those emotions myself either.

"Speaking of Valentine's Day, what sort of gift does a woman usually give a man?" I wasn't sure whether my boss and Molly were the right people to be answering this question, but the holiday was quickly approaching, and I needed ideas.

J.T. barked out a laugh. "I've got suggestions, but they're not suitable for discussing in the office."

I felt my face redden. "How about suggestions that aren't X-rated, then?"

Molly swiveled her chair to face me. "A card? Gourmet donuts? My mom gives my dad chocolate-covered cherries every year. He loves those things."

"A really nice bottle of wine?" J.T. said. "A set of barbeque tools?"

"That he can't use until this summer?" I wrinkled my nose. "Maybe wine. That might be a good idea."

"Ooo! Does he have a favorite movie?" Molly bounced in her seat. "Get a DVD of his favorite movie, and some gourmet popcorn, then make a little coupon about date-night being on you."

"That's a good idea!" I jotted it down, thinking that might just work. The judge and I both enjoyed watching movies together. There was a gourmet popcorn store in Milford. Yes, that might just work.

After a few other suggestions that ranged from personalized wooden carving boards to car detailing gift certificates, to whisky infusion kits, I felt better about my gift options. So far, I liked Molly's popcorn-movie-night one the best, but the car detailing certificate was a close second—especially since the judge had recently carted two crates of puppies around in his backseat.

That done, I got the puppies settled with food, water, and chew-toys, their leashes attached to the legs of the desks so they didn't wander off and get into trouble. Then I grabbed a cup of coffee and handed the sheets of paper with the potential puppy adopters over to Molly, asking her to use the form on Prucilla's website as a template to create one of our own, then e-mail it to the people on the list. There was no sense in doing any kind of reference or background check on them until we were sure who actually was serious about adopting one of the pups. After sleeping on it, the people who'd been so interested yesterday might have changed their minds.

I definitely intended on doing a background search on any potential applicants. Speeding tickets and misdemeanors were one thing, but I wasn't about to consider any applicant who had a history of violence toward people or animals.

That done, I went through the stack of work on my desk. Repossession. Suspected cheating spouse. Bail bond review. A custody case. J.T. had done most of the legwork on that one, but he wanted me to go through credit reports and comb through social media. I worked on that one for about an hour while trying to keep the puppies from chewing on my pants leg or the table leg. By noon I was far enough ahead I didn't feel bad about picking up Prucilla's planner and going through the last few weeks of appointments and notes. She'd meticulously written the times in the margins, and added comments to each appointment. On Friday, she'd met with three people, including a man named Ken Wollitt at four o'clock about a dog named Pepper. The word no was underlined three times along with a brief comment that he had no fenced yard and was "a bad fit." I did an internet search for anyone in a fifty-mile radius with that name, and printed out the social media picture of a Ken Wollitt in Milford.

Tommy Frys e-mailed me back while I was researching Ken Wollitt and confirmed a late lunch meeting with me at two-thirty.

My contact at the courthouse let me know that Lady's former owner was a woman named Pat Booker. Online court records showed nothing more serious than a few traffic tickets. There wasn't anything on social media or the internet that matched anyone by that name who lived in the area, and I doubted the Pat Booker I was looking for was a thirteen-year-old girl two states over who had a YouTube channel filled with videos of her violin recitals.

This wasn't going to be an easy person to investigate. I didn't exactly want to just knock on her door and grill her about the confiscation of her dogs, her feelings about Prucilla Downing, and where she had been Saturday afternoon between the hours of three and four. I'd need to figure out some other way of getting information about Pat Booker, and it would need to wait because I had a late lunch with Tommy Frys.

"I'll be back in about an hour," I told Molly as I gathered up my coat. "Can you manage the puppies until then?"

"Sure. And once J.T. gets back from the courthouse, he can help with them," she said.

I doubted that. J.T. was liable to flee to take care of a sudden, urgent errand if he came back and found he'd been nominated for puppy care. Molly was on her own. Thankfully, she seemed absolutely capable of juggling four rowdy puppies as well as her work.

CHAPTER 13

*I*t only took me ten minutes to get to Milford, and almost as long to find a parking spot and walk into the restaurant. A man seated at a back table waved me over, standing as I approached.

"You must be Kay. I'm Tommy." He put out his hand to shake mine, then waited for me to sit before returning to his chair.

Tommy Frys was not what I'd expected. When I was young, activists were lean with long, shaggy hair and a fervent, determined gleam in their gaze. The leader of Free the Fur was bald and clean-shaven with a gentle smile and kind eyes behind wire-framed glasses. When he'd stood to shake my hand, I noticed his shirt buttons were strained over his round belly.

"Thanks for meeting me," I said, quickly glancing over the menu.

"No problem. I can't believe Prucilla is gone." He shook his head. "She was outspoken, never one to back down from a fight, and ruffled more than a few feathers, but *murder*? I'm still in shock."

"Everyone is," I assured him.

The waitress stopped by our table and I ordered a black-bean burger with a side of cucumber slaw. Tommy got the hummus plate. I pulled out my notepad after she'd left and stared down at my list of likely suspects.

"Prucilla's niece asked me and my friend to find good homes for the nine puppies her aunt had taken in, but she hasn't hired me. I'm not working for her in any official capacity, nor am I working for the police."

Tommy tilted his head, a smile twitching at the corner of his mouth. "But you used to be an investigative journalist, and now you're a private investigator. You want to know who killed Prucilla Downing. I wouldn't expect any less from the woman who put our mayor in jail for murder and who solved the Holt Dupree case." He laughed as I blinked at him in surprise. "What? I Googled you. I'm sure you did the same with me."

"I did." I couldn't help but like this guy. "So tell me what's not on the internet. What was your relationship with Prucilla Downing?"

The man leaned back in his chair. "I met Prucilla twenty years ago at a dog show, of all things. I was in college, protesting with a group of my friends in front of the venue. She came out after showing her Boxers and we had a lively discussion about animal rights, and what she called responsible breeding. We disagreed about a lot of things, but agreed about more. We kept in touch, and when I started Free the Fur, she sent us our first donation."

"Sounds as if she was a mentor to you," I commented.

Tommy's gaze softened and focused into the distance, momentarily lost in memories. "Yeah. She always told me I was doing good things—important things. We never did agree on dog shows or dog breeding, but I learned to pick my battles. I'm vegan and ideally I'd prefer we not kill and eat animals, but Free the Fur works toward ethical husbandry and slaughter practices. Lobbying. Protests. Write-in campaigns to public officials. Articles exposing the ugly underside of what happens to produce our chicken tenders and ground beef." He shrugged. "Baby steps. Focus on quality of life and a swift, compassionate and respectful slaughter process first, then work on eventually reducing and hopefully eliminating our consumption of meat."

The waitress put our food down and I thought about what Tommy had said as I took a bite of my meatless burger —which was delicious. "Do you really think that will happen? A society of vegetarians, or vegans?"

He scooped hummus on a pita chip and ate it before answering. "Maybe not in my lifetime. Maybe not ever. But that's no reason not to try."

I ate a bit more, admiring the man's passion and commitment. In college, I'd wanted to change the world as well. It had been part of the reason I'd gone into journalism. But Tommy Frys really was changing the world, one animal at a time.

And Prucilla had been as well.

"That's our main focus," he continued. "But Free the Fur is about more than just the animals destined for someone's plate. Puppy mills, and pet stores are also issues we concern ourselves with. About nine years after I first met her, Prucilla formed Second Chance Rescue and started taking in and finding fosters and new families for Boxers. Soon after, she stopped showing and breeding and devoted herself full time to Second Chance. Within a few years, she'd expanded to taking in other dogs and began specializing in animals that had been seized for neglect or animal cruelty. She worked closely with animal control and rescue networks across the region. I'd let her know if Free the Fur was targeting a specific store or puppy mill, and she'd use her connections to coordinate the press reports, investigations by the local animal control, and assistance from rescues in the area. Over the years we've gotten thirty puppy mills and two chain stores closed down across the nation. Prucilla made sure there were soft places for all those animals to land once they were seized. She's saved a lot of lives, and ensured thousands of animals have had a second chance at a loving home."

Goodness, the woman really had been a saint. "Did Second Chance Rescue have something recent they were working on? Besides that local puppy mill case?"

Tommy frowned for a second. "Not that I'm aware of. Prucilla was always working on something, but I she wouldn't usually tell me unless it was a project where Free the Fur could assist. Things like getting dogs transferred to the rescue from out-of-state high-kill shelters, or running campaigns to help with medical expenses in neglect cases were a big part of what Second Chance Rescue did, and we didn't really get involved in that part of their operation."

I couldn't see a fundraiser for an injured dog, or transporting a dog from a shelter to the rescue would be the sort of thing to result in a murder. There had to be something else.

"Did you know if Prucilla was involved in other issues that might have angered someone enough to want to kill her? Or if she ever expressed any worries to you about someone? Was she being threatened at all?" I asked.

Tommy laughed. "Threatened? It happened, but it wasn't anything she took seriously. Applicants for her dogs would sometimes get really angry with her. She was strict about her adoption policies and didn't let her rescues go to just anyone. I doubt someone would have murdered her over getting turned down for a dog, but who knows?"

My thoughts went to Ken Wollitt. An argument, even one loud enough for a neighbor to have noticed, didn't seem to be enough of a motive for murder, but I still wasn't going to cross that name off my suspect list yet.

"Do you think the puppy mill guy might have killed Prucilla?" I asked as I checked my notes. "Rich Reed."

Tommy waved that suggestion away. "Nah. That guy's running a business. He honestly doesn't see dogs as any different from chickens on a farm. He's angry that we got him shut down and doesn't think he's done anything wrong, but I don't think he's the type who'd murder someone over it. Besides, he'd probably go after me rather than Prucilla. I'm the one who interviewed with the papers. I'm the one who stirred up the public opinion, that got animal control to finally act and seize the animals. Prucilla coordinated the rescues that took them in, but she wasn't the one hammering at Rich Reed's business like I was."

I checked my notes again. "How about the recent case with the animal neglect? Prucilla had a dog in a crate in her living room that had been from that case. Do you think that woman would have come to try to get her dog back? Maybe she and Prucilla fought, and the woman killed her?"

"The lady on Angler Road?" He shook his head and sighed. "There's no excuse for animal neglect, but I actually feel kind of sorry for that woman. She's got to be over eighty years old. She ran a cat rescue when I was a kid. She'd fundraise for tip-neuter-release programs and take in feral cats and strays that were not really adoptable. I think she's had some health issues in the last few years—mental as well as physical—and things just got away from her. She definitely should not have had all those animals in those conditions, but she didn't do it out of any sort of malice or greed. I believe she really wanted the best for the animals in her care, but just…couldn't manage."

It didn't sound as if this woman had been the type to murder someone. I knew some pretty spry eighty-year-olds, but I couldn't see any of them bludgeoning a fit middle-aged woman to death, breaking a dozen trophies and ripping up a fur coat, and managing to get it all done in half an hour before escaping out the back door just as Daisy and I were arriving. The woman Tommy had described didn't sound either physically, or emotionally, capable of murder.

"Besides," Tommy continued, "there were twenty dogs and thirty-five cats seized in that case and only one dog went to Prucilla's rescue. I don't even think anyone besides animal control, me, and Prucilla knew she had one of the dogs from that case. If that woman, in a fit of anger, wanted to get her animals back, she would have gone to animal control, not Prucilla's house."

I reluctantly drew a line through Pat Booker's name.

"Had Prucilla confided in you about *any* other case she was working on?" I asked, thinking about the Golden Retriever breeder. "Another puppy mill? A breeder neglecting their dogs? Some kind of potentially unethical situation?"

Tommy wrinkled his nose and hesitated a minute before answering. "You know, I think she *was* working on something. She asked me to be at her house last Wednesday when the transporters were due to arrive with that batch of puppies from a shelter in Kentucky. She wouldn't have missed that unless it was something important." He held up his hands. "It could have just been a doctor's appointment she couldn't reschedule, but knowing Prucilla, I'd bet it had something to do with her rescue business."

I jotted a reminder to look in Prucilla's planner and see if she'd put anything down on last Wednesday about an appointment.

"I'd heard she was thinking of going back to dog shows. To breeding pedigree dogs." I said casually, watching Tommy's expression carefully.

The man's eyebrows shot up. "Really? I wouldn't think she'd do that. It would take time away from the rescue, and that's been her passion for the last eleven years."

His surprise seemed genuine, but some people were good actors. "It doesn't bother you to hear that? You said you're against dog shows and breeding. Would it bother you if Prucilla had gone back to that?"

"I'd be disappointed, absolutely. But even after she gave up showing and breeding Boxers, Prucilla and I still had a difference of opinion when it came to those things." He shrugged. "I would have told her that she was making a mistake, that fewer dogs would be helped, be saved, if she had to divide her time between dog shows and the rescue. But I wouldn't be angry. I count—counted—Prucilla as a friend, and sometimes you need to accept that you won't agree with everything your friends believe in."

His words and reaction pretty much shot down my vague theory that she and Tommy might have argued over the issue, and that he'd killed her in a fit of rage over it. It was one more name to cross off the list.

I wouldn't be coming away from this meeting with a key suspect and the equivalent of a smoking gun, but Tommy had helped me learn more about Prucilla and narrow down the suspects I did have.

Right now it looked like the killer was that angry applicant, regardless of what Tommy said, or the murder had something to do with Prucilla's Wednesday appointment. I briefly wondered if it had to do with the Golden Retriever woman in Lakepoint, then decided that would be a stretch.

It *all* was a stretch, honestly. The police, with their resources, would do a better job catching the killer than I would. I knew I should let it rest and just focus on finding the puppies forever homes, but I couldn't let it go.

I paid the bill, thanked Tommy for his time, and was getting up to leave before I remembered one more thing.

"Oh! I almost forgot to ask you." I pulled the bag from my tote and opened it up. "Do you know if Prucilla would have worn, or owned, a coat made of this?"

Tommy recoiled from the fur sleeve, looking at me as if I'd yanked a dismembered corpse out of my purse in the middle of a restaurant. Although to a vegan, I guess I pretty much had just done that.

"I've never known Prucilla to wear furs or have them at all." He waved the item away, and I shoved it back into the bag. "She didn't believe in the same things I do, but a fur coat? Never."

"Not even if it was her mother's or grandmother's? Maybe she kept it out of sentimental value because a relative of hers used to wear it."

He shook his head. "No. I mean, I guess that's possible, but I can't see Prucilla doing that. There are other things to remember people by besides keeping a bunch of dead animals they used to wear stuffed in a back closet."

Well, when he put it like that, my theory sounded just horrible.

"If it had been her mother's or grandmother's, then she probably would have thrown it out," he continued. "Or better yet, sold it to Fillington's and donated the money somewhere."

I frowned. "Fillington's?"

He waved a hand. "Fillington's Vintage and Consignment Clothing. Downtown. On Main Street. They buy, and take in vintage clothing on consignment. There's a whole room in the back with coats and accessories."

Secondhand fur coats? I hadn't even known there was a market for that sort of thing.

If the coat hadn't been Prucilla's, then the killer must have brought it with them. I doubted a killer would have left incriminating evidence behind by slicing up their *own* fur coat, and the things probably cost thousands of dollars new. That was a lot to spend on a red herring.

I glanced down into the bag at the sleeve. My knowledge of furs was pretty close to zero, but this didn't look like it was new even *before* it had been sliced up and dumped at the scene of the crime.

I thanked Tommy once more and headed to my car, pulling my cell phone out to send Molly a quick text, telling her I'd be later than I'd originally thought. There was one more stop to make before I headed back to the office, and that was to Fillington's Vintage and Consignment Clothing.

* * *

PARKING ON MAIN Street was always a nightmare, so I pulled into one of the many decks and walked the four blocks to Fillington's.

Two huge glass display windows flanked the door. Headless mannequins wore clothing that stirred up all sorts of memories. One had a lavender linen pencil skirt with a matching boucle jacket. Another sported bellbottom pants in a bright sunflower print paired with a stretchy yellow tube top. I smiled, remembering the entire drawer of tube tops I'd once had back in the '70s. That was one particular fashion I had *no* interest at all in repeating.

Inside, the store had five long rows of hanging racks, all organized by decade, style, and size. A sign at the rear of the store informed me that coats, shoes, and accessories were in the back through another door.

"Can I help you?"

A woman about my age emerged from the racks, a smile on her matte-red lips. She wore a pair of high-waist, pleated, tweed trousers paired with a snug, cream turtle neck. I tugged at my sweater, feeling a little self-conscious about my lack of coordinated fashion.

"I was wondering if you sold secondhand fur coats, and how often people buy that sort of thing."

She laughed. "Not as often as I wish they did. We've got quite a few in the back. Is there a particular fur you're looking for? Full length or jacket? Or perhaps a detachable fur collar or a fox drape?" She eyed me. "I'm guessing you'd be a size eight, or perhaps a ten if you're thinking of layering it over a full skirt or a suit jacket."

"Actually, I'm hoping you can tell me if you recognize this coat. I've only got the sleeve. It was…uh, cut up." I pulled the bag out of my tote, reluctant to show her without warning after the last reception the thing got.

She came close and watched as I slowly removed the sleeve from the bag.

"Oh my! Poor thing." She took it in her hands and examined it. "It wasn't in the best of shape before, but it certainly didn't deserve this sort of treatment."

"So you recognize it?" I practically danced with excitement.

"I do. Normally I don't buy this kind of fur, but I felt a bit sorry for the man who was selling it. Most of what I have is mink, sable, or fox—or the occasional rabbit if it's a classic 70s coat or purse. As I said, it wasn't in great shape, wasn't a particularly aesthetically interesting style, and not many people want this fur."

"What is the fur?" I had no idea, and my mind was racing through all sorts of horrors. Was it from a dog? Had I been carrying around dog fur in my tote? It was bad enough that Prucilla was murdered, but for someone to have sliced up a dog-fur coat and thrown it at her feet? Her ghost should haunt that killer for the rest of their days for that.

The woman wrinkled her nose. "Coyote."

"Oh, thank heaven!" I blurted out. Coyote wasn't much better, but at least it wasn't a dog.

"I'm sure there are people who wear that sort of thing," she continued. "I mean, *someone* originally bought it. But it doesn't really fit in with what I carry here. I was surprised when it sold, but I'd priced it cheap and lots of times people come in here looking for items to use as costume or for reenactments."

Or murder, it seemed.

"Can you tell me anything about who bought it?" I crossed my fingers, hoping it had been the killer and not Prucilla, deciding she suddenly wanted to wear furs.

"A man." She laughed at my expression. "Some men like fur coats, and this guy was intrigued that it was coyote. He bought it last week as I remember. I don't think he signed up to be on my mailing list or anything. I could go through my receipts and see if he paid by credit card, but that coat didn't cost a lot. He might have paid cash."

I dug a business card out of my wallet. "Can you call me when you find out? Do you remember at all what he looked like? If you saw him again, would you recognize him?"

She tucked a stray lock of silver hair back into her bun. "Probably. He was in his late forties or early fifties and not very tall—maybe five-seven or five-eight? Dark hair that was combed back. Receding hairline. Not handsome, but not ugly either. He dressed in really plain—gray polyester pants that should have been hemmed up an extra inch. White button-down shirt with too much starch that looked like it was on its second day of wear." She grimaced. "I figured he was buying the coat for a play or his kid's costume or something because he sure didn't seem to be the sort of flashy guy who'd wear a fur coat himself."

I noted down her description, then reminded her to

please call me if she discovered the buyer's name. Thanking the woman for her help, I headed down the street to Poppin' Nation.

Since I was already in downtown Milford, I might as well get the gourmet popcorn for my Valentine's Day gift for Judge Beck.

Poppin' Nation was surprisingly busy for a Monday afternoon. I looked at the selections while the frazzled clerk helped the five people ahead of me in line. Personally, I preferred plain old buttered popcorn, but some of these flavors were intriguing. Caramel. Bacon cheddar. Buffalo hot. Ranch. Jalapeno and cheese. Salted caramel. Chicken and Waffles. A few had chocolate or caramel drizzled over the top. By the time it was my turn, I still hadn't decided which to get, so I ended up lugging a giant five-gallon tin with samples of every variety they sold to my car.

Popcorn? Check. I'd still need to figure out a good movie to buy or stream, and make a movie-night coupon, but getting those things done before tomorrow night was absolutely doable.

CHAPTER 14

"I'm sorry. I'm so sorry." I hustled into the office, tossing my things on my chair and shooting Molly an apologetic look. It was past four o'clock, I was behind on my work, and I'd abandoned Molly for hours with four rambunctious puppies. The floor was covered with pee-pads, shredded papers, chew toys, and bits of kibble. The water dish must have been knocked over at some point, because there was a pile of wet paper towels in the kitchenette sink.

"It's all good, but whew, this is really making me rethink any desire to have kids." Molly laughed. "I had to lock the trash cans in the bathroom, and they like to play in the water bowl. I think they're part retriever."

"Probably." I picked up Lacey and snuggled my face in her brown fur as she licked my cheek. Her breath smelled like puppy food.

"J.T. came back just after you left to pick up some files then promptly fled."

"Coward." I put Lacey down and sat at my desk. I still had that repossession to work on. J.T. would want that first thing tomorrow morning. I glanced at the clock, thinking I should text the judge and let him know I might not be home until six. Or maybe seven. Or I could go home on time and just do the repossession research after dinner. I'd much rather work at the dining room table with Judge Beck opposite me than be here late in an empty office.

"Here." Molly plopped a stack of folders onto my desk. "I got pics of each of the puppies to send to people so they could say which one they were interested in. I even had Daisy send me pics of hers to include. Ten people filled out applications so far including a friend of mine and that deputy friend of yours."

"Miles?" I hadn't thought he'd be interested in a dog.

"Yeah. He came by this afternoon to see if you had any muffins or scones." Molly rolled her eyes. "I swear that guy went into withdrawal when you were out skiing. He came by a few times with paperwork for J.T. and kept asking when you were coming back."

I would need to step up my baking game. Things had been so busy since we'd returned from our vacation that I hadn't had time to make my usual volume of baked goods. Hmm. I had the ingredients for muffins. Maybe I'd make a batch of red velvet ones in honor of tomorrow being Valentine's Day.

"Anyway. There are ten applications. I attached a picture of the puppy they're interested in to each one, along with a second choice if they indicated they had one. I also did a record's search for arrests and convictions and attached that as well as a credit check report. There's a yellow stickie inside each folder where I've rated the applicant on a scale of one through ten on how suitable I think they are." Molly's smile was downright smug. "There are six other applications still pending, so you might want to wait to make a decision, but I think we've got some good homes lined up for these guys."

Wow. I hoped she'd had time to get her actual work done, although knowing Molly, she probably worked straight through lunch. The girl always brought in a brown bag with a sandwich or leftovers, but I still felt guilty that she'd done all this when she should have been relaxing—although I guess it would have been impossible to actually relax with four puppies trying to eat the entire office.

"Thanks. This is amazing." I smiled at her. "I'll need to discuss all this with Daisy. She's kind of an equal partner when it comes to placing these guys."

I was sure the judge would want to see the applications as well, and probably the kids would, too. Maybe we could go over them after dinner. Then I'd make muffins. And work.

I did some preliminary work on the repossession case and took charge of the puppies while Molly did her skip traces. We worked a bit past five-thirty, then I packed my tote with my notes, the adoption folders for the puppies, and the work I wanted to get done tonight. Molly and I wrangled the puppies into their harnesses, and attached their leashes, then the girl helped me get them all situated in my car.

This wasn't easy. I'd miss them when they were gone, but having to deal with four puppies was *work*. I watched Molly drive out of the office parking lot, then put my car into gear, turning up the radio to drown out the cacophony of barking from the back seat.

I really needed to get these guys home and get dinner started, but I couldn't help but make a left when I should have made a right, heading out to Prucilla's house. I actually had hoped to catch her neighbor home, but was surprised to see Grace's car in the driveway.

"Stay here, and don't eat my car," I told the puppies who were jumping and crying in their cages thinking they were about to be let out.

Grabbing my tote off the passenger seat, I jogged up to a

neat split-level rancher and rang the bell. The woman who answered door was wearing a business suit, her hair pulled into a low ponytail and her feet in tennis shoes.

"I'm so sorry to disturb you, but I'm looking for Melissa Burns and I didn't know which house is hers?"

"I'm Melissa."

She opened the door a few inches wider, eyeing me with curiosity but not inviting me in.

"I'm a private investigator, helping Prucilla Downing's niece with a few things related to her aunt's death." I handed the woman a business card.

"Oh my gosh, I heard about that! How horrible." The woman glanced up and down the street. "We're a quiet neighborhood here. No problems. No trouble. I can't believe she was murdered right next door."

I nodded sympathetically "I'm helping to find adopters for some puppies she hadn't had time to place with a foster."

"I saw a bunch of people hanging up flyers on Sunday for a missing dog," she interrupted. "Did you find her?"

"We did. She's unhurt and safe, but I wanted to ask you about something else—a disagreement you witnessed on Friday between Prucilla and a potential adopter."

She laughed. "Wow, gossip spreads fast, although I'm not surprised. Yeah, I work from home on Fridays and saw them arguing. Actually I heard them and went out front to see what was going on. Prucilla always had a lot of people coming and going for her rescue business, but I'd never seen her have a shouting match in the front yard with anyone before. It was crazy."

"Could you hear specifically what they were arguing about?" I asked.

She nodded. "The man was trying to adopt a dog, and it sounded like Prucilla had told him no. He was cursing at her and calling her all sorts of horrible names. At one point it looked like he was going to grab her or hit her. He had his hands in fists and took a few steps toward her, but then he turned around and left. Got in his car and burned rubber leaving." She pointed to the road. "You can still see the skid marks."

Holy cow. Tommy might not have thought a rejected applicant would be angry enough to come back a day later to murder Prucilla, but after hearing this woman's story, I was starting to think this man might be the killer.

"Did you tell the police any of this? Has anyone come by to take your statement?"

She shook her head. "There was a card on my door from some detective when I got home from work today. I was about to call him when you came by.

"Definitely do," I urged her. "Make sure you tell him what you told me."

Her eyes widened. "Do you think that guy is the one who murdered Prucilla? I saw a murderer? I wonder, would he have killed her Friday if I hadn't been standing on my porch, obviously watching them? Oh my Lord, he came back the next day and killed her. What if he'd come to my house and killed me too?"

I waved my hands, trying to calm her. "We don't know for certain if the man you saw was the person who killed Prucilla or not, but it's important for you to talk to the police about this. One more thing." I pulled a piece of paper out of my tote and held it up for her. "Do you remember what the man looked like? Was this him?"

As soon as I'd shown her the picture, I wondered if I was screwing up Detective Keeler's case. If she identified this person without any other pictures as control samples, it might be a problem during the trial. She was upset, a little frightened...it would be terrible if she identified the wrong man.

Melissa frowned at the picture. "That looks like him, except the man I saw had a beard. It was around four o'clock on Friday. He was wearing jeans and one of those heavy tan coats. He was driving a truck—a pickup truck, not a work truck. It was a Ford I think. Red. It looked like a basic model, not one of the big diesel ones, or with a lot of chrome and extras on it. It was really clean and shiny. Kind of new—within the last three years I'd guess."

I jotted down some notes, surprised that the woman seemed to have paid more attention to the man's truck than the man himself. Then I thanked the woman for her help, reminded her to call Detective Keeler and tell him just what she'd told me. Once I left her house, I went next door to Prucilla's and knocked.

Grace opened and smiled when she saw me. "Kay! Please come in."

"Oh, I wish I could." It was already dark, past six o'clock, and I still had a ton of things to do including that research on the repossession case for work. "I'm in a bit of a rush to get home, but I wanted to give you a quick update. We've made some progress on finding the puppies good homes. I've got applications and background checks to go over, but I think most, if not all, of them will have loving, forever homes by next week at the latest."

"Oh, that's wonderful news!"

"Did you want to go over and approve final candidates on the puppies' adoption?" I asked her. "That way you can see which puppy is going to which home and weigh in on the applicants before we make any decisions."

She bit her lip. "I probably should. I mean, I trust that you and Daisy will have the best homes lined up for them, but I know my aunt would have wanted me to at least look the applications over."

I nodded. "I'll call you when we're ready. How are you holding up?"

She smoothed back a stray blonde hair. "Okay, I guess. I went in to work today, but left early and took a few days off to deal with everything. Mom is here helping—which is great because I really didn't want to stay in the house alone after what happened. There's just so much to go through, and foster families are calling, wondering what we're going to do about applications and the dogs they're caring for."

I remembered back to when Eli had died, not quite a year ago. There had been so much to do. Paperwork, and funeral arrangements, and people calling to offer their condolences. Going through his things had been especially difficult. Occasionally I would still run across something of his and feel that jolt down deep in my chest at the painful reminder that he was gone. "It *is* a lot, and having to deal with grief on top of it all makes it doubly hard."

She nodded. "How is Lady holding up, by the way? I'm so glad you all found her so quickly. I don't think my aunt would be able to rest knowing one of her dogs was lost and in danger."

"Lady has adjusted remarkably fast," I told the woman. "Daisy bathed her and clipped the mats out of her hair, so she looks different, but kind of cute with her new 'do. She mothers the puppies and is helping with the five Daisy is caring for. Oh, and she and the puppies all joined us for our yoga practice this morning." I chuckled, remembering how Lady had enjoyed romping in the backyard with the puppies, and how she'd jumped over Daisy's back.

"I'm glad she has Daisy," Grace said. "Mom and I will be here for the rest of the week, so call whenever you want to finalize any of the puppies' adoptions. Or just stop by."

"I definitely will." With any luck, I'd be calling tomorrow

or Wednesday about final adoption candidates for some of the puppies.

Lady had been found. The puppies would soon have new homes. And there was not only a solid lead in who might have killed Prucilla, there was a witness to an altercation between the two.

With any luck, everything would be wrapped up by the end of the week—including the murder case.

CHAPTER 15

The smell of Hunan beef and fried rice hit my nose as soon as I opened the door. Taco ran for my legs to attempt his usual escape, only to pause at the two cages of puppies blocking his exit.

"Kids! Go help Miss Kay with the puppies!" Judge Beck called from the kitchen.

Henry and Madison came from the dining room, the boy grabbing one of the cages and his sister the other. While the kids dealt with the pups, I put my tote and purse down on the foyer table and bent to pick up my cat. He bumped his head against my chin and purred.

"Your routine is totally thrown off, isn't it boy," I told the cat as I made my way into the kitchen. "Puppies everywhere, making noise and trying to eat your food. What's a poor cat to do?"

"Get extra meals out of it, that's what a poor cat is to do," the judge told me as I entered the kitchen. He was scooping Chinese food from containers into bowls and turned to wave a finger at me—or possibly the cat.

"Do not feed him. He's eaten twice tonight. I fed him as soon as I got home, then he convinced Madison that he was starving and that everyone had forgotten to feed him, so she gave him a second can of food. Bad kitty."

It was a never-ending battle to keep Taco's weight at the high end of the normal range. He begged for food and treats, counter surfed, made his way to all the neighbors' houses, trying to eat their pets' food and informing them that I was a terrible owner who was starving him to death. One look at the round cat with his glossy fur and they knew he was lying, but it was hard to say no to big green eyes and a plaintive meow.

"You all haven't eaten yet?" I asked as I put Taco down and went to wash my hands. It was almost seven. I'd expected to come home to leftovers, not them getting ready to sit down with takeout Chinese.

"Henry had a meeting after school for spring track-and-field and Madison was studying with a friend for an AP History exam. It was either takeout at seven, or we all just grab something on our own."

I'd learned over the last year that Judge Beck liked to sit down with his family for dinner. He'd worked so many long hours when the kids were little that dinner was sometimes the only chance they had to connect.

Ignoring Taco who was standing over his food bowl, insisting that no one had fed him, I grabbed plates and silverware, then set the table as the kids corralled the puppies in the powder room. They provided plenty of barking-music in the background while we ate and discussed our day. Madison was stressed about her history exam. Henry was excited about spring sports and promised to fix the broken porch chair this weekend. The judge had a jury selection on a trial. I avoided talking about my side-sleuthing on Prucilla Downing's murder and instead discussed Molly's and my progress on the puppy adoptions.

"I hate to see them go." Henry sighed. "I wish we could have a dog. Or all four. They're so cute."

"They're cute now, but in a few months when they're still having accidents in the house, chewing up your Nintendo controllers, and stealing your snacks, they won't be so cute," Madison told him.

"Don't act like you don't want one, too," Henry accused his sister. "You play with them all the time. You tried to sneak Cagney up to your room last night to sleep on your bed."

My eyebrows shot up at that, and I looked over to the judge.

"I caught her," he told me. "No non-housebroken animals in the bedrooms."

"I was going to bring some pee pads up with her," Madison protested. "She wouldn't have gone on my bed."

"Riiiiight," Henry drawled. "You saw how much pee and poop was on those pads in the morning. They're little. You wouldn't have woken up in time to catch her before she peed on the bed. Or pooped."

"We do not need to be discussing bathroom issues while eating." Judge Beck eyed his son with a stern frown. "Human, puppy, or cat bodily functions are not topics for the dinner table."

"How about bird poop?" Madison shot her father a saucy smile. "Or elephant poop. Or poop emojis?"

"No poop." The judge waved his fork at Madison. "No poop or pee or talk about any bodily functions in animals, vegetables, or minerals."

"Minerals don't poop," Henry chimed in. "Vegetables don't either."

"Eli used to talk about his surgeries at the dinner table," I told the kids. "It was gross at first, but you get used to it."

Judge Beck sighed. "Let's save all that for after dinner, okay? Please?"

"Okay." I smiled, feeling a little sorry for the guy. The kids and I were clearly ganging up on him here.

We went on to discuss non-gross topics for the rest of the meal. Once everyone had finished, the judge cleared the table while the kids and I got to work in the kitchen.

The doorbell rang, setting off another round of frenzied barking from the puppies.

"I'll get it," the judge called out.

I left the kids to finish putting away the leftovers and followed him, thinking it was Daisy here to go over the applications. Instead of my friend, it was Detective Keeler who stood at the front door.

Judge Beck reached out to shake the man's hand. "You here with a warrant for me to sign, Detective?"

The man's lips curled slightly upward. I didn't think I'd ever seen Detective Keeler smile, so the expression was a little unnerving.

"No, Your Honor. Not yet. I wanted to talk to Ms. Carrera, if that's okay." He sent a short nod in my direction but kept a respectful gaze on the judge.

"Of course." Judge Beck opened the door wider. "Come in. Kay, do you want to talk to Detective Keeler in the living room? We just finished dinner," he explained to the detective.

"I'm so sorry to have disturbed you." Keeler stepped inside, his astute cop's gaze sweeping my house and, I'm sure, missing nothing. I probably could have blindfolded the man and he would have been able to tell me every single item in the room down to the dust on the windowsill.

I led the detective into the living room while the judge headed for the kitchen to give us some privacy.

"I just finished speaking with Melissa Burns," Keeler said, not bothering with small talk. "When she said she'd had a private investigator visit her, I knew it was you—even before she showed me the business card you'd given her. I've said this before and I clearly need to say it again, Mrs. Carrera: Stay out of my case."

"Please take a seat, Detective." I motioned toward the sofa. "Can I get you some tea? Coffee? I'm sure the judge has put on a pot."

His glower lessened with the mention of Judge Beck, and he shot a quick, worried frown toward the kitchen. I knew I wasn't getting the full brunt of the detective's anger and frustration because of my roomie. There were rules in the world of law enforcement, and evidently "don't yell at people in a judge's home" was one of them.

"Ms. Burns told me about the argument the decedent had on Friday afternoon with an applicant for one of her rescue dogs," the detective said, ignoring my offer of a seat and refreshment. "She said that you showed her a picture of someone she positively identified as the man."

Keeler glared at me as he said this, and I smiled serenely back. I had something the man wanted. I'd gone through Prucilla's planner, found the names, and researched them myself. I'd done the legwork that the busy detective hadn't had time for yet, and he wanted the fruits of my labor.

I was happy to oblige, but not before yanking his chain a bit.

"I'm just a nosy lady. Just someone meddling in your case. You've probably already discovered the name, address, phone number, and date of birth of the applicant Melissa Burns saw arguing with Prucilla Downing. There's no way a skilled police detective such as yourself would need the help of little ole me."

He rolled his eyes. "Don't start that nonsense with me, Ms. Carrera. You're a licensed private investigator. And even before that, your snooping did help in solving several murders in the county. This is not something you're being paid to investigate, and I don't want you sticking your nose in the case, but as a citizen who cares about justice, I would expect you to share anything you've discovered about the murder of Prucilla Downing with me."

He was right, and I felt a bit guilty about stalling when there was a murderer walking free in our county. Pulling the sheet out of my tote, I handed it over to the detective, telling him that I'd found the name from Prucilla's planner and done an internet search.

"A jogger in the neighborhood told me Sunday about the argument, and gave me the name of the neighbor who'd witnessed it," I said. "We were all out hanging up flyers for the missing dog."

Detective Keeler looked at the paper before folding it and putting it in his pocket. "Thank you very much for this. And *please* tell me you didn't go see this man and confront him."

"Not yet," I assured him. "I had to get home for dinner, and I didn't want to go by myself to talk to a possible murderer who'd last been seen cursing and yelling at the victim in her front yard."

I'd been thinking of asking Judge Beck to go with me, although I knew he'd probably tell me to let the police handle it. Daisy would have gone with me. Between the two of us, I doubted Ken Wollitt would have been able to bludgeon either of us to death.

"Do *not* talk to this man." Detective Keeler scowled at me. "Do not. Do you understand me, Ms. Carrera? Whoever killed Prucilla Downing is dangerous, and I don't want another murder up on my board to investigate. Got it?"

"I understand," I told him, promising nothing.

I hadn't had time this evening to go question Ken Wollitt,

what with puppy applications and my work to catch up on. By tomorrow, I was pretty sure the man would already be either in police custody or in an interrogation room. Actually, by the steely glint in the detective's eyes, I doubted he'd wait until morning to question the man. Ken Wollitt was probably going to have a very bad evening.

CHAPTER 16

$\mathcal{I}$ saw Detective Keeler to the door, promising to convey his goodbyes to the judge. Once the detective's car had left my driveway, I heading into the kitchen to find that Madison, Henry, and Judge Beck had finished with the dishes.

"Go do your homework," the judge said to his kids after glancing at my face.

After a few grumbles from the pair, they left us alone, heading up to their rooms with their backpacks.

"So...?" Judge Beck leaned against the counter, his arms crossed.

"I spent a good bit of the day digging around on the Prucilla Downing case," I admitted. "There were a whole lot of dead ends, but I ended up talking to a neighbor of Prucilla's who witnessed her having an argument with an applicant for one of her rescue dogs. It looked like it might have been close to turning violent from what the neighbor said."

The judge let out a long breath. "I'm glad you told Keeler. While I'm one hundred percent in support of your sleuthing, I would sleep better at night if you left the confrontation and arrest of suspects to those who are carrying guns on their belts."

"You're probably right." I ran a hand through my hair. It was eight o'clock. I still had work to do on that repossession case, some baked goods to make to appease Miles, and Daisy was due over here at nine to go over puppy applications.

Judge Beck took a step forward, putting his hands on my shoulders. "Just be careful, Kay. I don't want anything to happen to you."

"Me either." I smiled up at him. "So…what do you have planned for tonight? Want to help me make some red velvet cupcakes?"

He laughed, stepping in closer. "Only if I can take some in to work. Deanna has been pestering me to bring pastries in since you made those espresso-glazed scones last month."

"Then get the muffin pans out and preheat the oven to three-fifty," I told him.

Red velvet cake had always been a favorite of mine. My grandmother's recipe had been a cherished heirloom in our family. They'd been moist and buttery, with a smooth burst of vanilla sweetness and a hint of dark cocoa, contrasting with the mild tang of cream cheese frosting. Red velvet cake had been a staple at potlucks, barbecues, and birthday parties when I was growing up. I'd converted the family recipe into one more suitable for cupcakes, and loved it just as well.

Plugging the mixer in, I grabbed the butter that had been softening on the counter since this morning and got to work. The key to good red velvet was butter. The cake had to be moist, but it also had to be buttery. The recipe had cocoa, but just a bit, because at the end of the day, this was a vanilla-flavor dominated cake.

Buttermilk. White sugar, because the molasses in brown sugar would overwhelm the vanilla and hint-of-cocoa flavor. Baking soda, just like Grandma's recipe had used. And vinegar. Judge Beck raised his eyebrows when I put the bottle of white vinegar on the counter with the other ingredients, but Grandma had known this was the secret ingredient for red velvet cake. Vinegar brightened the food coloring, making the cake traffic-light red. And we'd always used cake flour, because the added cornstarch produced the small, delicate crumb so iconic to this cake.

The judge and I got to work, our movements synchronized as we made the batter and poured it into the prepared baking tins. While the cupcakes baked, I shooed Judge Beck off to check on his kids while I made the cream cheese frosting.

The doorbell rang just as I was taking the cupcakes out of the oven. I set them on the rack, put the cream cheese frosting in the fridge to cool, and went to answer the door.

Daisy had her hands full—literally. All five pups were in harnesses and leashes, and had completely tangled themselves together. Lady was looking smart in a blue and white striped sweater, the close-cropped fur and outfit making her look less like a terrier and more like a small whiskery greyhound.

I took the puppies from Daisy and began untangling them while she removed the leash and sweater from a very calm Lady. My pups were greeting their siblings with a barking frenzy and I'd barely gotten the harnesses off Daisy's before the whole nine were off and running.

"So much for barricading them in the powder room." I sighed. Now that the puppies knew how to escape their area, I was liable to come down in the morning and find my house trashed with chewed upholstery and poop everywhere.

"Lady has already figured out how to open doors. I put all their crates in my bedroom, thinking having me nearby would quiet them down, but nooooo. I wake up to find Lady

149

in my bed and all the puppies loose and running around the bedroom."

"Just hang in there," I told her as we walked to the dining room. "With any luck, most of these guys will be in their forever homes by the end of the week."

"I'll miss them, and I know Lady will miss them too, but it'll be nice when it's just the two of us. It's hard to bond with Lady with five puppies in the house." Daisy eyed the folders strewn across the dining room table, her gaze snagging on Prucilla's planner. "Any progress in finding the killer?"

I gave her the abbreviated version of what I'd discovered, along with a quick recap of Detective Keeler's visit this evening.

"You weren't really going to go over and try to interview that suspect, were you?" Daisy asked as I handed her half of the folders.

"Not without backup. It's all moot now, anyway. Detective Keeler will take care of it. My only job is to find nine puppies their forever homes." I sat across from her and opened the first folder. Out of the corner of my eye I saw Daisy regarding me with a skeptical expression.

"What?"

"Ten bucks says you'll check arrest records first thing in the morning, call the courthouse, and probably bribe Miles with muffins or scones to tell you what's happening."

"Red velvet cupcakes," I corrected her. "I'm bribing Miles with red velvet cupcakes. The police might be handling the murder investigation, but that doesn't mean I'm not curious. If Ken Wollitt killed Prucilla, then Keeler will have him in jail within the next day or two. Probably by morning. I just want to make sure they've caught the killer."

"And if it's not this Ken Wollitt?" Daisy asked.

I shrugged. "I don't know who else it might be. There's always a chance that someone else from Prucilla's past might have wanted her dead, but if so, I would think she'd have been uneasy and suspicious and told her sister or her niece or someone."

"But she let the killer in the front door," Daisy countered. "If Ken Wollitt was cursing and screaming at her on the front lawn, why would she have let him inside the next day? I would have slammed the door in his face and called the police."

Me too. And that was one thing that bothered me about this. Even if he apologized and seemed calm, why would Prucilla have let him inside? She wasn't going to allow him to adopt a dog from her, no matter how contrite he seemed. Why let him in, lead him into the living room, then turn her back on him?

She should at least have been wary of the guy, struggled and fought back, and not trusted him to be behind her, let alone in her house. The killer was someone she didn't think would be violent. And from what the neighbor had said happened Friday afternoon, Prucilla knew Ken Wollitt could be violent.

But I didn't have any other suspects. What I did have was nine puppies—all of which needed good homes.

Daisy and I went through each of the applications, writing down our approval numbers in different color ink next to the ones Molly had given each candidate. Then we sorted them by puppies and averaged out each score.

I held a handful of folders in the air. "These are rated the highest by all three of us. And, of course, they all want your puppies."

"If mine get adopted out, I'll take some of yours," Daisy promised. "It wouldn't be fair for you to be stuck with four and for me have zero—especially since I'm the one who got you into this mess."

She was the one who'd pulled strings at the shelter to get

custody of these little fur balls. But there had been no way Daisy could handle nine pups and a new rescue dog. Of course I helped her. That's what friends were for.

"So it looks like we have homes for Pancake, Biscuit, and Apple." I smiled at Daisy's use of food-names. "We also have two 'possible' applications for Oatmeal, and one 'maybe' for Nutmeg."

"I want to wait and see if we get some other applications in before taking another look at those," Daisy said. "That one family who wanted Nutmeg looks good, but I want to ask them about their yard. And I really want to do interviews and site visits with all of them before we finalize the adoptions."

I handed over the folders. "You go ahead and call these and arrange to visit their homes since they're interested in your puppies."

Daisy eyed the other folders. "How about yours? Any good candidates for your detective squad?"

"There's one I want to talk to about Lacey. And Miles told Molly he might be interested in Hutch. I'll talk with him tomorrow and get a firm yes or no on his interest."

"I'd love it if they could go to people we knew." Daisy reached down to scratch the top of Lady's head. "I've gotten kind of attached to the little guys. It's going to be hard to see them go."

And it would be a whole lot easier if we got to see the puppies now and then. Miles would probably bring Hutch by the office to visit. And he was dating Violet, who had been coming to our happy hours. I'd need to make sure she brought Miles next time, along with the puppy.

It made me wonder about other people I knew who might be interested in adopting one. Olive and Suzette had Gus. Kat and her husband had a dog, and I didn't think they were interested in adding another—especially when they were running a bed-and-breakfast out of their house. Matt Poffenberger? Carson and Maggie? Heather had seemed interested. Although she'd said she really didn't have time for a puppy, the kids were there every other weekend and it wouldn't be a problem for the judge and me to puppy sit on and off.

There was a good chance that four to six of the puppies would go home in the next two days. That would only leave us with three to five puppies to place. Molly had said there were several pending applications she hadn't yet passed along to me. If those panned out, then these puppies might all go home by the weekend.

It was with a mixture of sadness and relief that I saw Daisy and her canine crew out, and put the folders back into my tote. We were well on our way to wrapping up puppy adoptions. Detective Keeler was most likely arresting Ken Wollitt right now for the murder of Prucilla Downing. And I still had research to do on that repossession case before I could even think of going to bed.

It was going to be yet another late night.

CHAPTER 17

$\mathcal{T}$he next morning's yoga practice was just as chaotic as the day before. Our poses might not have been perfect, but I actually enjoyed having puppies running in between my legs and arms, and Lady occasionally sprawled out right where I needed to place a foot or hand.

Having Madison and Henry here made the morning routine a bit easier. They were up earlier than usual, waking without the customary prodding from their father. Henry immediately got started on the puppies' breakfast while Madison scrambled eggs and made toast for us all. By the time I came down from my shower, four puppies and Taco were eating away and breakfast was on the table.

"Happy Valentine's Day," Madison said with a smile as she scooped eggs onto the plates.

"Thank you for cooking this morning, Madison," I told her as I sat down. "And thank you, Henry, for taking care of the animals."

"He's trying to show dad that he can take care of a pet so he can keep one of the puppies," Madison said.

"We have a cat," Judge Beck informed his son. "We don't need a dog, and even if we did, Taco wouldn't approve."

"Taco likes the puppies," Henry countered.

"That's a bit of a stretch," I told him. "Taco tolerates the puppies because he can steal their food."

"Okay, Taco tolerates the puppies," Henry corrected. "Besides, we could have the dog at mom's when we're there, so he'd only be here every other week."

"How do *you* feel about this?" the judge asked his daughter.

Madison shrugged. "They're cute. I'd love to have one, but I'm going to college in less than two years, so I'm not going to be the one having to take care of a dog long-term."

It was a good point. She'd be gone in two years, and Henry would be off to college himself in another four. These puppies could live another ten years after the kids were gone. I wasn't sure I wanted that responsibility, and I wasn't sure Heather or the judge would either. I didn't want them to feel pressured into taking on the obligation of a dog to make their kids happy. I'd seen how both of them were quick to give in, both trying to make up for the pain of the divorce with special vacations, and even a car as Madison's Christmas present. Would they acquiesce and adopt one of the puppies, only to regret it later?

"Speaking of college, how are the applications going?" the judge asked.

Madison wrinkled her nose. "I wish I didn't have to apply to so many places. There's an essay I have to write for each one, and mom says I can't just use the same one over and over."

"Because each college is asking you to write about something different," the judge reminded her.

"Not really. It's all 'write about someone who influenced you' or 'write about a pivotal point in your life' kind of thing.

I could write one essay and tweak it." She glanced hopefully over at her father. "Or just apply to one or two colleges instead of six."

"The two you really want are a stretch." Judge Beck waved a finger at Madison. "If you don't get accepted at those, you'll be scrambling to fill out last-minute applications to others that might have already filled their freshman class."

"Then I'll take a gap year like they do in England. I can do volunteer work for a year or travel. Chelsea is going to Europe for a year. She's going to backpack around, stay in hostels. That sort of thing."

"You are not backpacking around Europe at the age of eighteen." The judge scowled. "Absolutely not. And especially not for an entire year."

"If you want to do volunteer work, you'll have all summer before college to do it," I told Madison. "Daisy and I can put together a list of organizations that would be thrilled to have a young, energetic person helping them out."

Madison sighed dramatically. "I'm going from high school straight to college, then straight to graduate school, then into the workforce where I'll slave away for the rest of my life. I'm just asking for a gap year to have fun, to be a child for one last time."

Judge Beck snorted. "You will have had eighteen years to be a child, and if you pick the right career, you won't be *slaving away* for the rest of your life. If you really want to travel, I'll support a semester abroad while you're in college, and as Kay said, you'll have plenty of time to do meaningful volunteer work in the summer after your graduate high school. I'm saying no to the gap year. And your mother and I are on the same page with this, so don't go complaining to her."

Madison shot me a quick glance, and I put up my hands. "Don't look at me. I'm not getting in the middle of this."

"I'm not sure I'm even going to go to college." Henry laughed at his father's stunned expression. "Kidding! I'm just kidding."

"Trade schools are an excellent alternative," I pointed out. "Bob Simmons down the street runs a HVAC company. And Phil Tennison is an auto mechanic."

"I had Phil go over Madison's car when I bought it," Judge Beck spoke up. "Kay is right, trade school is an alternative."

Henry nodded. "I thought about carpentry, about fixing and repairing antiques, but making that record cabinet was *hard*, and it's still wobbly on the one side."

I reached out to pat his hand. "Well, you did a great job replacing that broken glass and the chipped tile, and I'm sure you'll do a wonderful job on that broken porch chair as well."

Judge Beck looked at his watch. "Finish up, kids. If we don't get moving, you'll both be late."

Henry rose and started to gather up the puppies, getting them sorted in their cages for transport. I began to clear the table. Madison stood and walked over to her father, planting a kiss on his cheek.

"I'll drop Henry off at school. That way you can have a little extra time this morning, and maybe help Miss Kay with dishes and getting the puppies in her car."

The judge looked up at her in surprise. "Thank you. I appreciate that."

Hmm. Breakfast. Offering to drop her brother off. What was going on here?

Then Madison surprised me by walking over to kiss me on the cheek as well. "See you tonight, Miss Kay."

"Drive safe, and see you tonight." I watched her walk out of the dining room, then turned to see Judge Beck doing the same.

"What's she up to?" he mused.

"I was wondering the same thing," I told him. What *was* that girl up to?

* * *

J.T. SIGHED as I struggled to carry two cages of puppies inside the office door. I was pretty sure each of these dogs had gained five pounds overnight, because they certainly hadn't been this heavy when I'd brought them in the house last night.

"Some of them have adoptions pending," I told J.T. as I filled bowls with water and food. "At least three of Daisy's and one of mine—two if Miles decides he wants one."

My boss looked relieved. "Are they going home today? Please tell me they're going home today."

"I doubt today, but with any luck they'll be in their new homes by the weekend." I held up my crossed fingers. "Daisy has to do home visits and interviews, and I don't think she can do three of those in one day—not with having to work."

He sighed and looked at my pups who were pawing at their cages and whining to be let out. "What if I pay Miles to take two? Or all nine?"

"Oh, stop." I laughed. "I know you're not happy about all these puppies, but you're scoring major points with Daisy for being tolerant and understanding."

"It's important to her," he said. "A little inconvenience on my part is no big deal if it pleases her. Although I will do a happy dance once these guys are all adopted out."

I snorted at the mental image of J.T. doing a happy dance.

"I finished up the repossession research last night." I set down the water bowl and dug in my tote for the folder. "Here. I highlighted three places where the owner might be hiding the car."

His expression brightened. "Well then I'll be gone all day, trying to find a car and take it in."

Which would leave me with the puppies—well, me and Molly as soon as she got in.

"That's fine. Just don't get shot." I was glad J.T. handled this side of the business. People got pretty angry when someone tried to repossess their car or truck. Although he'd never been actually shot, J.T. did have stories of a few people threatening him with a shotgun, or trying to physically drag him out of their vehicle.

J.T. grabbed his jacket off the chair. I held off letting the puppies out, waiting for him to leave first. Once he was gone, I slid the bolt on the crates and let loose the hounds—or whatever they were. Molly would need to knock to get in once she was here. I didn't want to risk one of the little guys escaping as she opened the door.

There was a knock on the door promptly at nine. I herded the puppies to the side of the office and opened it to see Miles Pickford on the other side, not Molly.

I stuck my head out and glanced to either side of him. "I've got the goods you're looking for. Come on in, but make it fast. You need to be out of here before the cops come."

His eyes widened. "You're feeding other cops your muffins and scones? Kay, how could you? I thought I was the only one."

I was sure Miles was absolutely unaware of the naughty innuendo of what he'd just said. He was a young cop, only a few years out of the academy and full of innocent optimism about his job and the public he served. I'd come to see him as sort of an adopted nephew and had been thrilled when he'd asked Violet Smith out. I'd been even more thrilled when that one date had turned into a relationship.

"I'm a dealer, Miles. My muffins are available to everyone." Oh my. That sounded even worse than what he'd said.

"You'll always be my first and favorite junkie, though," I assured him.

Miles walked in, then immediately garnered my approval when he veered away from the table with the cupcakes to pick up Hutch and give him a quick cuddle. Baked goods were usually a priority for him, but clearly puppies came first.

After petting the dogs, Miles washed his hands in the sink while I poured him a cup of coffee and slid one of the red velvet cupcakes onto a paper plate.

"So? What are your plans for tonight? Given that it's Valentine's Day." I asked, deciding I'd press him about his potential adoption of Hutch later.

A wide, sappy grin split his face. "It's our first. Violet and I are going down to that Bavarian place that is always booked up two months in advanced. I made the reservations a few weeks after we started dating, hoping things would work out with us. Anyway, it's a drive, and I'd like us to have some wine and relax, so I got a hotel room down there. Fancy one with a big king-size bed and little chocolates on the pillows at night. I made sure Violet took tomorrow off, but she doesn't know where we're going."

"That sounds wonderful!"

He clearly wasn't going to be taking Hutch in the next few days, even if he'd decided he did want to adopt the puppy. Not that it would be a problem. The kids would be home, and I knew they'd happily take care of Miles's pup for him.

"Actually." He dug in his pocket, his face turning an interesting shade of tomato-red. "I know we haven't been going out long, but I was thinking of giving Violet this."

He produced the iconic little velvet-covered box and flipped it open to reveal a ring with a small round diamond solitaire.

"Is this okay? I mean, it's not fancy or anything, but it's a good quality diamond."

My eyes filled with tears. "It's perfect. Classic and timeless. I hope she says yes."

"I hope so too." Miles wiped his brow with the side of his forearm, then closed the box and stuck it back into his pocket. "I love her. She's smart, and beautiful, and I can't imagine my life without her."

Darn it, I was totally going to cry. I knew Miles had initially had some doubts about dating Violet. She was amazing, but her family wasn't so amazing—especially for a cop. Her parents and siblings had been in and out of jail her whole life. Her youngest sister, Peony, was still in juvie for manslaughter and a host of other charges in the death of football star Holt Dupree. And although Violet wasn't like the rest of her family, she loved them very much and marrying her would mean he would be spending holidays and rubbing elbows with the very people he might be arresting the next week.

"I hope I'm invited to the wedding," I told him. "You are an amazing couple."

"She's an amazing woman, and I'd be lucky to have her as my wife." Miles picked up the coffee. He looked down at Hutch, who was jumping on Cagney and growling playfully and chewing on her ear. "I talked to her about this little guy. She approves, so I think I want to go ahead with the adoption—if it's okay with you and Miss Daisy, and if you'll hold him until this weekend to give me time to get supplies."

I couldn't help doing a quick hop in excitement. "Then he's yours. And we'll definitely hold him until the weekend. Madison and Henry are with us, and they've been so helpful with the puppies."

"A fiancée and a dog." He grinned sheepishly. "Well, hopefully a fiancée. She hasn't said yes, yet."

Again, I teared up, thinking of the fresh-faced cop and Violet, the woman with big dreams of forensic accounting who'd overcome a rough childhood to go to college and score a good job at the courthouse. They'd be starting their life together, much as Eli and I had done decades ago.

A young couple. A puppy. A little starter house in the 'burbs. Kids.

Time was a wheel, turning and shifting, with everyone having their ascent and descent, their rise and fall. Seeing Miles with that ring in his hand made me remember my own ascent. I didn't regret where I was in life—not one bit—but I enjoyed seeing others come along to enjoy the love, life, and family that I had enjoyed. That I still enjoyed. Out skiing, Madison had asked me about my lack of children, and it had made me think about that time in Eli's and my life. We'd shifted course when we'd been unable to conceive, building a life that was no less rich, but just different. Still, I loved seeing my friends and my friends' children with little ones of their own.

Someday this would be Madison and Henry. I hoped they continued to talk to me about their hopes and dreams long after college, marriage, and kids.

"Any information on the Prucilla Downing case?" I asked Miles. I hadn't even had time to check the list of last night's arrests, but I knew he'd be up on all the gossip at the station.

He grinned. "You know we're not supposed to talk about official police business, Kay—especially an ongoing investigation."

"I didn't ask Detective Keeler, I asked you." I handed him the cupcake, knowing that baked goods were Miles's weakness. "Don't make me spend hours this morning finding out on my own. I used to be an investigative reporter, you know."

"A skill that translates well to your new job." Miles took a bite of the muffin and I waited while he lost himself in the taste. "Wow, these are awesome. They taste just like my grandma's red velvet cake, only smaller."

Not the most poetic compliment in the world, but I'd take it. In general, being compared to something his grandma made was high praise.

"The case?" I reminded him.

"Mmmmf." Miles chewed and swallowed before answering. "Keeler brought a man in for questioning late last night, but there are no arrests yet."

I frowned and thought about that. Keeler was cautious, and so was the prosecutor. I knew the detective would want a solid case before he made an arrest, but I'd have thought there was enough evidence to at least hold Ken Wollitt.

"He had an alibi?" I guessed. Taking Miles's silence for an affirmative, I continued. "He might be lying. He was there Friday afternoon. A witness saw him in a loud argument with Prucilla. His demeanor was threatening, and he even took a step toward her as if he wanted to turn their argument physical. It has to be him."

I'd poked my nose into enough murders in the last year that I knew it didn't have to be Ken Wollitt. Yes, the obvious suspect was often the killer, but that wasn't always the case.

Miles leaned in closer to me. "The guy's alibi is a room full of fifth graders and their parents. He was at his kid's birthday party at an indoor bounce-gym an hour north of Milford. The party ended about half an hour before you and Daisy discovered the body. He wouldn't have been able to drop his kid off at home and make it there in time to commit murder, and Daisy spoke to Prucilla while the guy was in the middle of the party, so he couldn't have done it beforehand."

From the neighbor's description of the confrontation, I'd been sure the killer was Ken Wollitt. As disappointed as I was, it seemed the angry man wasn't the killer.

"He has a kid? An eleven-year-old kid?" I wondered. It

didn't fit the image I'd put together of the man yelling and cursing at Prucilla in her front yard, but even parents lost their temper.

"His daughter really wanted a dog for her birthday." Miles quickly finished off the cupcake and reached for another. "He'd spent an entire week talking to Prucilla, filling out applications, even had a home visit. He said after all that, a day before his daughter's birthday, Prucilla decided she didn't like the chain-link kennel he'd put in his backyard and refused to let him adopt a dog. He was frustrated, felt like he'd been strung along, and got mad. The guys who were at the station when he was being interviewed said he seemed embarrassed about the whole thing. He claimed he didn't even know she was dead and thought he was being brought in because Prucilla had taken out a restraining order on him or something."

"Wow, you guys really *do* talk over the coffee pot," I commented.

Miles nodded. "Murder's a big deal around here. Someone gets killed in the county and we all want to know what's happening."

Me too. I'd clearly misjudged Ken Wollitt. The angry man who I'd pegged as the killer had just been someone past his limit of frustration, someone who'd lost his temper and regretted the outburst. And I felt bad that he hadn't gotten one of Prucilla's dogs. Had the woman been too strict about her adoptions? I glanced down at the puppies romping around the office and wondered if I was being too strict as well.

"Evidently he and his daughter spent Sunday going around to animal shelters so she could pick out her own dog." Miles took a sip of his coffee. "Guy said it was probably for the best since his kid has a dog she really loves. The cops there during the interview said he seemed genuinely shocked to hear Prucilla had been murdered."

And there went my primary suspect in the case. Not that I really had time to be solving a murder case, what with my regular work and all these puppies. Keeler was a good detective. He'd find the killer, and he'd do it just fine without my help.

"I wanted to ask you a few other things." I took a deep breath, then plunged right on in. "Did you all take the trophy from Prucilla's that was an award for an owned-and-bred dog? It wasn't the one with the blood on it—the one I assumed was a murder weapon."

Miles thought for a second, then shook his head. "I only saw one trophy being bagged up, but I wasn't there the whole time and haven't seen the evidence log. If there were prints on another item, they might have taken it."

"And blood?" I asked. "Besides Prucilla's that is. Lady didn't have any blood on her muzzle when we found her, but I was thinking that maybe she bit the killer?"

Miles shrugged. "We took a lot of samples from the scene, but haven't got the labs back yet. You know, with these sorts of murders, there's splatter. Most of what we found is probably the victim's, but that's something Keeler would know more about than me."

I frowned, knowing I wasn't going to get any answers out of the detective.

Just then, the door opened and Molly rushed in. "Sorry I'm late. My alarm didn't go off this morning."

"It's okay," I assured her. It wasn't like she hadn't worked late last night, and I knew Molly didn't often write down her overtime. "I brought red velvet cupcakes."

"And they're amazing," Miles told her. "Just like my grandma's."

That praise earned the officer an extra two cupcakes to-go. Miles left, and I got down to work, alternating my research with cleaning up puppy messes and keeping the furry monsters from chewing on desk legs. I also squeezed in time to call the woman who'd wanted to adopt Lacey and arrange for a home visit. If that adoption worked out, there would only be four puppies left to find homes for—two of mine and two of Daisy's.

"Kay?" Molly spun around her in chair and nervously extended a folder. "Here's another application for a puppy. Starsky. The solid black one."

I took it from her and glanced inside. "This is…you?"

She bit her lip and nodded. "I thought about it overnight. Hunter and I talked about it. Between the two of us, we'd have more than enough time to take care of a puppy. He works different hours than I do, so someone is almost always at home. And I like the idea of having a dog there when he's out making late deliveries and I'm home alone."

I was thrilled. Molly would be the perfect puppy owner. She'd proven herself to be patient and loving with them here in the office, and I knew she'd be just as patient and loving with Starsky at home. This meant we were down to only three puppies needing a home.

"I think Starsky is a good match," she went on. "He's not as rambunctious as the others. He's kind of lazy and chill, and loves to curl up in my lap and sleep when I'm working here."

"I don't think he's going to fit on your lap for long," I warned her. Daisy had guessed that the puppies would end up around forty pounds. I was pretty sure that would put them above the lapdog range.

"Oh, I know, but he can still snuggle up beside me on the couch at home." She reached down and picked the puppy up. "I checked my lease and we're allowed to have a dog or cat and there are no weight or breed restrictions. I just have to pay a pet deposit and a little extra each month. I know I don't have a backyard, but the apartment complex has a little grassy area where people walk their dogs, and between Hunter and I, he'd get lots of exercise."

I thought of Ken Wollitt, and of Prucilla's insistence that his dog run in the backyard wasn't good enough, that adopters needed a fenced yard. But I'd rather have a dog go to a loving home with people who were actually going to take it for walks and spend time with it as opposed to just letting it out in the backyard all by itself.

And I knew Molly and her brother. I knew they'd be wonderful dog parents. I'd been by her apartment a few times in the last month to drop things off for work and knew it was large enough for a pup that might grow to forty pounds.

"I'll need to talk to Daisy, but I don't think she'll have any objections," I told the young woman. "Go ahead and start buying supplies because you're probably going to have a new puppy in the next twenty-four hours."

Molly squealed, pumping her fists toward the sky and sending all the puppies into a riot of excited barking. "Hunter will be thrilled. I'm going to send him a picture. Sit here, Starsky. Sit. Can you sit for me? Good boy!"

I turned back to my desk, filing Molly's application in my tote and getting started on the day's work. At noon I got a call from the woman who'd been interested in Lacey asking me if I could come by around two-thirty. I jotted down her address, then worked through lunch since I'd be leaving early. I completed the paperwork for one of our bail bond clients, faxed it to the courthouse, and was filing the folders when I noticed Prucilla's planner sticking out of the top of my tote.

I had nothing. No leads on the case whatsoever. Tommy Frys didn't have any reason to kill Prucilla. He'd made a convincing argument that the puppy mill guy, Rich Reed, wouldn't have wanted to kill her either. Lady's owner wasn't physically capable of that sort of thing. Ken Wollitt had an alibi. Had Prucilla met with anyone else who might want her dead? Did that planner hold the clues that might point me to her murderer?

If not, the planner might point me toward potential adopters for the three puppies that still needed homes.

I took an hour and carefully went through the book, deciphering Prucilla's often illegible handwriting. After handing off a couple extra names for Molly to call and inquire about potential interest in one of the remaining puppies, I once more noticed last Wednesday's entry about the Golden Retriever breeder in Lakepoint. There was no name, no phone number, just the scribbled line and a date.

Why had Prucilla gone to see her? Was this the breeder listed on the internet with the photos of happy dogs romping with children on a grassy lawn? Surely the woman who owned that kennel wasn't suspected of neglect or animal cruelty? Maybe Prucilla had contacted her about being a foster? Or she'd asked the woman for a donation to the rescue? Grace had said that she'd heard from her mother that Prucilla was thinking of going back into showing and breeding. Perhaps she'd decided instead of Boxers, she'd switch to Golden Retrievers, and had gone to talk to the woman about possible upcoming litters of puppies?

There was only one way to find out. I needed to go see Lacey's potential adopter, and it wouldn't take much more time to drive to Lakepoint and visit this Golden Retriever woman. I'd just leave work early and put in some extra time tomorrow. Today was Valentine's Day, and I needed to make sure I was home on time, for once.

CHAPTER 18

The glossy website photos didn't do Victory Lake Goldens justice. The place was actually a small farm on about ten acres. White buildings with red roofs dotted the property. Neat rows of metal fencing jutted out from either side of two of the buildings. As I pulled up, half a dozen barking dogs dashed out the door flaps that separated the indoor part of their kennel from the outdoor side. The website had said Victory Lake did grooming and boarding of all dogs, as well as breeding "quality Golden Retrievers for family and show households." The business looked to be well run and organized, but as I parked, I wondered if Prucilla had discovered something not quite right under the professional veneer—and that was what had gotten her killed. I'd heard of unethical breeders and puppy mills whose websites and Facebook pages made them appear wholesome, while underneath the false front, the dogs suffered. Victory Lake *seemed* to be what they'd touted on their website, but I couldn't help but have my suspicions.

I left my car, went through a door marked "office," and

was instantly overwhelmed by the noise of barking dogs, clippers, and vacuuming.

"Can I help you?" A smiling woman behind the counter shouted over the din.

"I'm looking for Vicky Ellinger," I shouted back, asking for the woman the website had listed as the owner.

"That's me." She grimaced and waved toward the door. "Let's talk outside. We've got six Doodles we're trimming in the back and I can't hear a thing over the noise."

I nodded and waited for her to round the counter before following her out. Vicky Ellinger was younger than I'd thought—mid-twenties at most. Her straight, reddish-blonde hair was pulled into a tight ponytail, and her face was makeup free. A long, light blue smock with the kennel's logo emblazoned on the upper right covered her khaki pants and plain T-shirt.

We stood outside, the noise dampening as the door closed behind us. The dogs still barked, but at least I could hear myself think without the sound of clippers and vacuums rattling my brain.

"I'm Vicky Ellinger." The woman wiped her hand on her smock before extending it to me. "What can I do for you? Are you here to book a grooming appointment? Boarding? Or about the wait list on our spring litter?"

"Actually none of the above." I hesitated, wondering if I should just get right to the point, or dig a little. "I had some questions about your operation. Do you have time to talk?"

"I can spare a few minutes." Her gaze narrowed. "Wait—are you doing an article? Or are you with that Free the Fur group? Because if it's the latter, I don't have time for you."

"You've had problems with Free the Fur?" I asked, skirting her questions.

She blew out a breath. "Who hasn't? My place is clean, my animals are healthy, and I treat every one of my dogs as if they were my children. Yes, I show dogs. Yes, I breed pedigree Golden Retrievers, but all my dogs are genetically tested and my litters carefully planned to produce the healthiest puppies with the best temperaments. I get that there are a ton of dogs in shelters, but those dogs aren't coming from us, they're coming from random backyard breeders—people who want cute little Fluffy to have some adorable puppies, even though Fluffy came from a pet store and a puppy mill, and she's got a congenital liver shunt, a heart defect, and a genetically inherited, partially collapsed trachea."

I stared wide-eyed at her rant, but she continued.

"Showing and breeding dogs? It's not a money-making enterprise unless someone is running a puppy mill and doing it at volume with low costs. There's genetic testing. There's the stud fee to get the perfect sire for the pups. There's medical care during the pregnancy, medical care for mother and pups afterward. There's shots and check-ups, and specialized food. There's sleepless nights hand-feeding the runt because you just can't bear to lose any of those little lives, no matter how much it might eat into your already slim profits. If you're lucky you have that one-in-a-million dog that wins big at Westminster—the one that everyone wants to breed to—but when you balance that one windfall across decades of careful breeding expenses and time, you'll be lucky if you end up breaking even. It's a labor of love. We do this because we're passionate about dogs, passionate about bettering the breed. That's it. The boarding and grooming pays the bills here. The Goldens? I'm not getting rich breeding and showing Golden retrievers. I do it because I love them. I do it because I know when someone buys one of my puppies, they're getting a healthy, wonderful addition to their family. I do it because there's one or two puppies in each litter that I think are exceptional and worthy of producing future exceptional litters. That's why I do it. And those Free the Fur people should go picket a slaughter house feedlot or a puppy mill and leave responsible breeders like me alone."

"Wow." That was really all I could manage to say at the moment.

"I'm sorry." She smiled sheepishly. "I didn't even get your name and here I am lecturing you. It's just been a week, you know?"

Yes, I knew. It *had* been a week, and it was only Tuesday.

"I'm Kay Carrera with Pierson Investigations and Bail Bonds. I'm here because I wanted to ask you a few questions about Prucilla Downing."

She took a step back. "Do I need a lawyer? I heard she was murdered. You can't seriously think… I barely knew her."

"*How* did you know her?" I asked. "There's a few scribbled lines in the book she used as a planner, but nothing to say why she might have contacted you."

The woman stared at me for a moment, chewing her lip.

"I'm not with the police," I told her. "I'm not here to arrest you or anything. I'm just tying up a loose end. My friend was adopting a rescue dog that went missing when Prucilla was murdered, and we were the ones who found her. We're helping her niece place some puppies for the rescue. Prucilla's planner had names and numbers of potential adopters, including a few others. Your kennel was listed, and I was curious as to why."

She hesitated another few seconds. "I'd only met her once —that day she came out to talk to me. I think it was Wednesday last week. I knew *of* her, though. When I was a kid, we'd sometimes run into her at the bigger dog shows. She was local, so my mom would always go over and say "hi". And I knew about her rescue, of course."

I sat on a nearby bench and motioned for Vicky to do the same. "Were she and your mother close?"

Vicky plopped down beside me. "Not really. Dog show people just kind of know each other. They didn't show the same breed, or even in the same group, but because we were local she and mom knew each other enough to nod and say hi. Then Prucilla stopped showing and got really involved in her rescue. I don't think she and my mom ran across each other after that, or had reason to speak to each other. But mom wasn't why Prucilla came to see me. She wanted to talk about my grandfather."

That was not the answer I'd expected at all. "Your *grandfather*?"

She smiled. "He passed about ten years back, when I was in high school. He'd been sick for a while, but when you're a kid, you never really expect death."

"Did Prucilla know him?" She must have, or she wouldn't have come to talk to Vicky. Had this just been her wanting to reminisce? Had Vicky's grandfather maybe been an old flame or something like that?

Vicky laughed. "Everyone knew Grandpa. He was kind of famous in the dog-show world. Remember when I said sometimes you get lucky and breed that one-in-a-million dog? That was Grandpa. Wilmont's Heart of a Lion was twice Best in Breed at Westminster, and came close to Best in Show once. He cleaned up at the other national shows as well and even was invited to Crufts. Lion was like the Secretariat of the dog show world. Everyone still talks about him."

I frowned because I'd heard that name before. Where had I heard that name? "Lion was a Golden Retriever?"

She shook her head. "French Bulldog. Mom showed them, too. I'm the one that broke with tradition and went with Goldens. I've always loved the breed, even as a kid. Started showing them at ten. It made for a chaotic household with Mom's Frenchies and my Goldens all running around. But Lion is the dog that made Grandpa famous."

"That's where I'd heard the name before." I chuckled. "Your grandfather's dog is *still* famous. My friend, Olive, just bought one of Lion's progeny. She's getting back into showing."

Vicky's smile was nostalgic. "Well, she can't go wrong with a pup from Lion. He always bred true. A good number of the big winners in the breed are out of his line."

"Was Prucilla looking at getting back into showing, this time with Frenchies instead of Boxers?" I asked. It was a good explanation for why she'd come to speak with Vicky about her grandfather's outstanding dog. "Perhaps she wanted to buy one of Lion's descendants from your mother?"

"Mom's been gone for two years this June," Vicky said with a sigh. "She retired from dog shows when I was in college and stopped breeding. I think when Grandpa died, she kind of lost interest—especially since I was showing a completely different breed. She kept her Frenchies until the end, though. I've got the last of her girls in the house. Trixie's ten years old but still going strong. They're great dogs. Your friend Olive is lucky to have gotten one from Lion. She probably paid a fortune for that puppy."

"She did," I assured her. "And she was thrilled to have a pup sired by such a famous dog, even so many years after he's been gone."

Vicky smiled at me. "Mom kicked herself for selling off that frozen semen after Grandpa died, but she knew she was only going to be breeding and showing for a few more years and wanted to make sure it was all used to further the breed. And she got a nice sum for it all, too."

"I'm sure she did." I forced my thoughts away from Olive and Gus and back to the reason for my visit. "Did Prucilla know your mother had passed? I guess if she wanted a puppy from Lion's line, she'd need to contact Denny Topper with Fairwoods Kennel."

"That's what I told her. And I let her know that if Denny had puppies from Lion, she should probably snatch one up right away. I'm sure there's hardly any of that semen left after ten years. Grandpa preferred to do live breeding, so he'd only frozen thirty straws when Lion was alive. There were only twenty-four left when Grandpa passed, and mom sold them as part of the estate."

I nodded, deep in thought. It sounded strange, but Prucilla *must* have been getting back to showing and breeding, only this time with Frenchies instead of Boxers. I couldn't imagine how she'd manage that along with the rescue, and it seemed weird for her to change her mind and go back to that after so many years. But people did change their minds. Olive hadn't participated in dog shows in almost a decade, but was going back to it. Maybe Prucilla missed the camaraderie, the competition. Maybe after so many years of seeing neglected and abandoned dogs with genetic disorders, she wanted to do her part to produce the best of a breed.

It was a shame she'd been killed before she could return to something she must have loved. She and Olive and Suzette would have been competing against each other at dog shows. Maybe they all would have become friends, sharing grooming tables and giving each other rides or something.

I thanked Vicki for her time and left, thinking about puppies, dog shows, and winner's trophies as I drove to the house I hoped would be Lacey's new home.

$\mathcal{I}$ knew as soon as I met the applicant for Lacey that this would be a good home for her. There were two girls, ages twelve and fourteen, who were already puppy-proofing the house. They excitedly showed me around as their mother put on a pot of tea. After I'd had the tour, I sat with Rachel and we discussed their family routine, the puppy's exercise needs, and crate training.

"It's mostly all hardwood floors here." She waved a hand around the house's open floorplan. "So any mistakes can easily be cleaned up. And if my old furniture survived the girls, then it will survive a little chewing by the puppy."

"We've been using pee pads, so housebreaking shouldn't be *that* hard," I told her. "Lacey is smart. She'll take well to obedience classes, if your girls are interested in doing that sort of thing with her."

Rachel nodded enthusiastically. "I already inquired about nearby classes. The girls are so excited."

I finished my tea and stood. "You all seem like the perfect family for Lacey. I need to swing by the rescue tomorrow to review your application with them. It's just a formality so they can sign-off on the adoption. I'll text you afterward to confirm, then hopefully I'll be able to bring Lacey by the next day so you all can meet her. If everything goes well, I can finalize things then, and she'll be yours by Thursday night."

"That would be amazing!" Rachel said.

Rachel and the two girls showed me out. I looked at my watch and swung by the florist and a candy shop, then hurried back to the office to retrieve the puppies.

* * *

I PULLED into my driveway promptly at five, brought in the puppies, and got them situated before I went back out to the car for everything else. I left the flowers and card for Eli in the car, and brought in the two heart-shaped boxes of candy I'd picked up for the kids before returning to wrestle the five-gallon can of popcorn out of the trunk. Back inside, I quickly attached the bow I'd picked up, as well as the coupon I'd made.

Arranging everything on the dining room table, I dashed upstairs to get ready for my big date. I was just coming down the stairs when the front door flew open and Henry dashed into the house.

"Whoa!" he exclaimed, seeing the assortment of goodies on the table.

"You and Madison each get a heart full of candy," I told him. "The popcorn is for your father. And if you're lucky, he'll share some with you."

Henry picked up both hearts, handing one to Madison as she came in. "These are from Miss Kay," he told her.

"Happy Valentine's Day," I said, giving each of them a hug. "Just make sure the puppies don't eat any."

"Thank you." Madison took in my dark gray sweater dress and black boots. "You look nice, Miss Kay."

"Dad ordered pizza delivery for us," Henry announced. "He's getting the fl—getting something out of the car."

"Idiot." Madison rolled her eyes. "You're not supposed to tell her."

"Don't call your brother an idiot." The judge walked through the door, a huge bouquet of roses in one hand and his briefcase in the other. "Happy Valentine's Day, Kay. These are for you."

"They're beautiful." I took the flowers from him. "Your gift is on the dining room table."

"It's popcorn," Henry announced.

I put the flowers in a vase while the kids sampled their candy. When I came back into the dining room, the judge had opened the envelope with the coupon I'd made and was reading it.

He waved the coupon. "So, I get to pick between Like Water for Chocolate, Pride and Prejudice with Colin Firth, The Bodyguard with Whitney Houston, Dirty Dancing, or Roman Holiday."

"I'm open to other movie suggestions, but I thought you'd enjoy one of those."

"And we get to eat the popcorn while we're watching the movie?" he asked.

I laughed. "Well, not all five gallons of it. Hopefully the kids will help us with that. And we can have some before we watch the movie if you want. I'm especially intrigued by the ranch-flavored popcorn."

He smiled at me. "You're making me look bad, Kay. And here I just brought you a bunch of flowers."

"Roses," I corrected. "And you're taking me out to dinner. Both of which probably cost ten times what I spent on that popcorn and streaming a movie."

He walked over to me. "I mean creativity. This is so thoughtful, and fun. Just like you are."

With that, he put his arms around me and pulled me close. I hugged him back, my face against his chest. His shirt was scratchy from starch, his body lean, muscular, and warm against mine. I breathed in the citrus-and-spice of his aftershave and the lavender of laundry detergent, and wanted to stay in his arms.

But we had dinner reservations, and something to do before that.

"You look wonderful. I like that dress." His voice rumbled in his chest. "Are you ready? We should probably get going soon."

I pulled away. He looked wonderful as well—but he always did, whether he was wearing a suit for work, jeans for the weekend, or khakis if he was heading to the golf course.

"I'm absolutely ready. I just need to get a few things from my car to take with me."

"Have fun," Henry shouted.

"Don't rush home," Madison added. "We've got pizza on the way, chocolate, and puppies. Stay out as long as you want."

The judge got my coat and helped me into it. He waited as I got the flowers and card from my car, holding the passenger door on his SUV for me, and shutting it once I was all tucked in. We were silent as we drove to the cemetery, but it was a companionable silence. I directed him where to go to find Eli's grave and was a bit surprised when he came around to let me out after he'd parked.

I walked through the brown grass to the gravesite while the judge stood by the passenger side of the SUV, waiting. Kneeling down, I arranged the flowers in the grave vase attached to the headstone, then wedged my homemade card in between the two. Blinking back tears, I ran a finger over the engraving.

"I miss you," I said, trying to hold back the tears. "I miss you so much. I think about you all the time. Sometimes I get sad, wishing you were here with me, but we had good times together, and remembering those times brings me a lot of joy."

I glanced back at the judge, then faced the headstone again. "I think you'd like the judge. He's smart and kind and has a good sense of humor. He's a good father. He's a good man, and I...I like him. We're going out to dinner, but I wanted to come here first, to bring you flowers and a card, just like you always brought me. I wanted to wish you a Happy Valentine's Day, and tell you that I love you. And I miss you."

I sniffed, wiping a hand under my eyes and composing myself for a moment, then I turned and waved the judge over. He came to stand beside me, and I reached out to take his hand, entwining my fingers in his. We stood there for a moment, both of us looking down at the grave.

"Are you okay?" the judge asked, concern in his voice.

I knew then that if I told him I wanted to cancel dinner tonight, he would. If I told him I wanted to be alone in my grief, he'd be silent and supportive as he drove me home. Anything I wanted, or needed, and he'd do it for me, be right there for me. I loved that about this man, and I knew Eli would have wanted that for me.

"I'm absolutely okay." I smiled up at him and squeezed his hand. "Except I'm starving. Let's go to dinner."

He smiled back. And the whole way to his SUV, we held hands.

CHAPTER 20

Judge Beck had made reservations at a little Italian place in downtown Milford. The restaurant was in an old brick rowhouse on Main Street. Diners ate in the downstairs rooms of the converted house, giving the whole experience an intimate feel. The candles, painted wall murals, and the Frank Sinatra music added to the charm. The eggplant parmesan I'd ordered was so good that I practically licked the plate, and Judge Beck's shrimp scampi was equally tasty. I knew because he'd given me a bite. I'd let him have a bite of my eggplant parmesan as well. Feeding each other samples of our dinner from our own forks was probably just as cheesy as the wall murals and Frank Sinatra music, but this was a holiday that was meant for cheesy.

After dinner, we walked along the downtown streets, the judge's arm around my shoulder. We stopped to listen to a street musician, admired the various Cupid sculptures that were part of a competition among the downtown merchants, and browsed the stores that had stayed open late for the holiday.

I paused outside of Fillington's Vintage and Consignment Clothing as we started to walk past, thinking once more about the fur coat.

"Do you want to go in?" the judge asked.

"Sure." I could check to see if they'd found anything out about who purchased the coat, and maybe I'd buy something. Vintage clothing wasn't really my thing, but I did love old jewelry, and I'd noticed some cute purses when I'd been in earlier this week.

The same woman was working tonight, this time wearing an A-line dress with an orange and red swirly pattern on the fabric. Her hair was up in a French twist, her lipstick still that iconic matte red. She looked up at us as we entered, her eyes widening in recognition when she saw me.

"Oh! Hello! I haven't had time to go through those receipts for you yet. It's been a week. Valentine's Day, you know." She waved a hand at the red and pink heart streamers decorating one wall.

The judge turned to me in surprise. "Receipts?"

"She might have sold the fur coat that the killer cut up when Prucilla was murdered," I whispered to him before turning back toward the woman. "But we're actually here to browse. Valentine's Day, you know."

The woman's gaze sharpened, and she quickly took in Judge Beck's expensive coat and shoes before rounding the counter. I remembered her incredible eye for detail when it came to clothing and knew that she'd just sized my date up and was hoping for a big sale.

"Did you want to look at coats? Purses?" She eyed the judge again. "Jewelry?"

"Jewelry," I told her. "And can I see that leather tote in the window? The brown one?"

"Of course." She waved a hand toward the jewelry counter. "Broaches and earrings are there. Necklaces are two rows back. Go ahead and take a look, and I'll get that tote out of the window."

I made a beeline for the counters, and immediately fell in love with the big, gaudy, paste-jeweled broaches.

"My grandmother had a pin like that." I pointed to one that was shaped like a daisy bloom. It was huge, at least two inches in diameter. And it was only fifteen bucks.

The clerk set the tote on the counter and pulled the tray of broaches from the case. I picked up the daisy one, thinking how fun it would be to wear on my spring coat. It was a bit louder and kitschier than the one my grandmother had worn, but I loved it.

I told the woman I'd take it, then the judge and I had a bit of a tussle over who would pay for the pin. I won, managing to hand over the cash first. Then as the clerk boxed it up, I turned to the tote.

Right away, I knew this bag was way out of my price range. Way, way out of my price range.

It was beautiful, though. I picked it up, noting the faint marks on the buttery-soft leather. This bag had been loved, but gently loved. It had a structure to it that would make it much better than my tote for carrying files and my laptop back and forth to work without the huge size and stiffness of my old briefcase. I glanced inside to see pockets lining the sides and a divider down the middle that had a zippered component and loops to hold pens.

"It's a Coach," the woman told me as she handed me a little bag with the boxed-up broach inside. "A limited anniversary-edition tote. They only made so many of these, and people don't sell them very often so they're hard to find. The ones you see listed on eBay and online marketplaces are usually fakes."

"It's beautiful," I told her as I returned the tote to the counter.

"Do you want it?" the judge asked me.

I laughed. "I'm not spending seven hundred dollars on a bag. Maybe I should go find one of the fakes."

"They won't hold up like this will," the shopkeeper warned me. "The leather on those fakes is cheap and shoddy, the stitching poor, the lining thin. *This* is the type of tote that will last you a lifetime. New, it sold for over a thousand dollars. It's a bargain at seven hundred."

I'm sure it was, but I still wasn't spending that for a bag. I had a tote, even though it wasn't ideal. I also had a briefcase. It would be a silly indulgence to buy another bag, and an extravagance to pay so much for one.

I thanked the woman, and we left. As we walked up the opposite side of the street, heading back to the SUV, my hand brushed against the judge's. With only the slightest hesitation, I snaked my fingers in his.

Holding hands. I felt like a teenager walking down the street like this, that giddy sensation stirring like butterflies in my chest at the feel of his hand in mine.

"Are you sure you don't want that bag?" Judge Beck asked. "You've got a birthday coming up next week. I could get it for you as an early gift."

He knew when my birthday was. But as sweet as the offer was, it didn't feel right for him to spend *seven hundred* dollars on a gift for me. Christmas had been extravagant, and I could guess how much he'd spent on including me on the ski trip, but I didn't want our relationship to start out like this. Eli and I had been poor college kids, and our first gifts were simple, heartfelt, and inexpensive. Judge Beck wasn't poor, but that wasn't the point.

"It's nice, but I don't think I want it. I'd constantly be worried about spilling coffee on it, or scratching it, or having it stolen." I squeezed his hand. "Although if you find a cheap knock-off on eBay, I won't say no."

"The fakes are never as good as the real thing," he said. "You'd regret it once it fell apart in less than two months."

"Not like I'd regret spending *seven hundred* dollars on a tote," I teased. "That's a furnace repair. A car repair. A new dryer. I can't drive a name-brand bag back and forth to work if the alternator goes out in my car." I stopped on the sidewalk and held up my other hand as I sensed him getting ready to protest. "And no. It's not any different when it's your money. Do not buy me that tote. If you do, I'll just return it and put the money toward the kids' college funds or something."

His lips twitched. "Okay, okay. No seven-hundred-dollar accessories. I get it. Be prepared to act surprised and delighted when you get a new dryer for your birthday, though."

"I won't need to act," I told him. "The surprise and delight will be genuine if you get me a new dryer."

He chuckled. "Heather would have killed me if I had ever bought her an appliance as a gift."

I stepped closer, sliding my arm against his. "Don't get me wrong, I'm a sucker for flowers and jewelry, too. But I appreciate gifts and actions that help to make my life easier. To me, that's more important than flashy, expensive presents, or even words of affection. Someone that sees what I need, recognizes that I'm stressed, or could use a little help, and just pitches in? That's everything to me."

Eli had been that way. If there had been dishes in the sink, he'd just done them. Laundry basket full? He'd do the wash. He made sure the oil was always changed in my car, that any squeak or rattle was fixed. When I was swamped at work, and feeling annoyed over having to cook dinner, I'd come home to find Eli had taken charge, or if he was equally swamped at work, had ordered carryout. He'd always known what I needed and just done it for me. Whether that was washing my car on a Saturday, buying flowers when I felt down, or saying "I love you" right when I needed to hear that the most. I loved being pampered just as much as anyone else, but it was the little, considerate things that truly meant love to me.

We chatted about all sorts of things on the drive home—Madison's college prospects, Henry's spring track-and-field meet schedule, how nice it would be to have the downstairs powder room puppy-free again, if it was really going to snow this week.

The house was dark and quiet as we pulled in. Even the puppies were unusually silent as we tip-toed through the front door. The judge's hands were warm on my shoulders when he slipped my coat off. I watched him hang both my coat and his in the closet. When he turned back, we both stood there for a moment in awkward silence.

We'd been holding hands, hugging, touching in little affectionate ways for almost a month now. Something had changed today. It had changed when I curled my fingers in his as we stood at Eli's grave. It had changed as we'd walked down Main Street, his arm around my shoulder.

I was all for slow romance, but we needed to move a little bit faster than this.

Taking three steps forward, I reached out and gripped his suit jacket with both hands, then looked up at him. "Thank you for tonight. I had a wonderful time."

The judge clearly knew an invitation when he saw one. With a quickly mumbled "you're welcome," he bent his head to mine and kissed me.

It was soft, gentle, lingering. Hopeful. His lips left mine and paused. We shared a breath. His arms slid around my waist, and as he pulled me closer, he kissed me again. The second kiss was deeper, more purposeful. I felt warm, breathless, and so very alive. Stepping into his embrace, I pressed myself against him, sliding my arms up over his shoulders to link around his neck.

Ack. Ack, ack, ack.

We jumped apart at the unmistakable sound of a cat barfing. Taco stood two feet away, heaving and then finally upchucking something that I really didn't want to identify onto the foyer floor.

"I think Taco disapproves." The judge laughed.

"I think Taco got into the puppy food again," I corrected him. "I doubt he cares if we kiss or not. Taco is only concerned about food, head scratches, and that no one steals his sunny spot on the window seat."

Either way, the spell had been broken—temporarily, at least. We'd explore this new territory in our relationship later, when there weren't two kids upstairs that might interrupt us at any moment—and when there wasn't cat puke on the floor.

CHAPTER 21

"So...how did things go last night?"

Daisy was asking this while we were both in a one-legged downward dog pose with barking puppies and Lady racing all over the lawn, so I gave her the abbreviated version of the judge's and my evening.

"It was romantic," I said at the end of my summary. "But it didn't feel forced. Everything with him is just so...comfortable."

That wasn't the right word. Generally, things *were* comfortable between us. But increasingly there were moments that weren't so comfortable. Each time we advanced our relationship forward, we had to break through awkwardness and uncertainty, but we did break through, and the increasing intimacy was easier the second time around. It was no big deal for us to touch now, to hold hands. It felt right every time he put his arm around me. And as for our kiss last night, well, we'd quickly become comfortable with that.

I liked these little displays of affection between us. I

hadn't realized how important a caring touch was to me until I'd found myself without it.

"Did you both get it on? Mattress mambo?" Daisy moved into a plank position.

I felt my face heat up at the thought. "With his kids here? Absolutely not. Besides, we're a little early in our relationship for that."

Daisy twisted her head sideways to eye me with raised-eyebrows. Given the glacial pace her and J.T.'s relationship had taken, and the amount of angst she'd spent over the physical side of things, she had no right to be giving me that look.

"We kissed." There. That was more than enough sharing for me, even though Daisy was my best friend.

"And?"

She stared at me, remaining in the plank. My abs were killing me. My arms as well.

"Then we kissed again. And we probably would have maybe gotten a little busy if Taco hadn't puked on the floor right beside us."

Daisy laughed, collapsing her plank onto the mat. It might have been unintentional, but I followed her move, happy to *not* be in a plank pose any longer.

"Well, J.T. and I had a wonderful dinner out. He spent the night, but I think that part of the evening wasn't up to expectations with five demanding puppies and Lady—who isn't quite sure if she likes J.T. or not. She kept escaping her crate and jumping in bed with us, trying to shove J.T. off the side and onto the floor."

A jealous dog. Hopefully Daisy would be able to set some firm rules with Lady going forward. That or perhaps invest in a king-sized bed.

"I did interviews and visits for the three applications we

approved and the two maybes," Daisy said as she moved into a cobra pose. "I liked all five. Once Grace gives her approval, I think these little pups are going to be off to their new homes."

It would be bittersweet. Just as bittersweet as saying goodbye to the ones I'd been caring for.

"I can take the applications over to Grace for you," I told Daisy, mirroring her cobra pose. "I've got three of my four ready to go. I really liked that lady and her two daughters who wanted to adopt Lacey. Miles wants Hutch and Molly wants Starsky."

"Molly will be a wonderful puppy mom," Daisy said, shifting back into a downward dog. "She did great with my five and Lady last night."

"She's been just as great with my four during the day at work," I told her, following her pose. "I just don't understand why no one suitable has come forward for Cagney, though. She's so cute with her light brown fur, and black mask and ears. She's sweet, loving, and friendly."

Once Grace signed off on the applications, all the puppies would be going to their homes, except for Hutch, who would need to stay an extra day until Miles and Violet got back from their trip. After that, it would just be Cagney, and my heart ached for the little puppy. I didn't mind taking care of the pup until we found the perfect family and home for her, but I still felt bad for her. After tomorrow, she'd be all alone, missing her brothers and sisters with only a grumpy food-stealing cat to keep her company.

Daisy and I finished our yoga routine, then bundled up for coffee outside as we watched Lady and the puppies play. Lady would miss these little guys, too, when they were gone. Plus, Daisy would need to start walking her to make up for the exercise she was getting now by chasing the pups around.

After our coffee, Daisy left, and I went inside to shower and get ready for work. The chaos of earlier in the week had already settled into a routine, and I came downstairs to find Madison toasting up bagels and Henry feeding the pups and Taco. I refreshed my coffee, grabbing another mug when I heard the judge's footsteps on the stairs.

He came into the kitchen. Our eyes met, and as silly as it sounded, it did seem as if time stood still for a moment. He walked forward, his arms coming up as though he wanted to embrace me. Then he stopped, hesitating a moment. I shoved the coffee at him, feeling awkward. Did we hug in front of the kids? Kiss? Did they know there was something growing between their father and me? Did the judge want them to know?

"Thanks." He took the coffee, then shifted his weight awkwardly from foot to foot. "I really enjoyed last night."

"Me too," I told him.

"Me too," Henry chimed in. "I ate all my candy, hung out with the puppies, and played video games all night. You guys should go out more often."

"It was fun," Madison agreed. "Next time I want to have a friend over, though."

"Can I have a friend over, too?" Henry asked before shoving a bagel into his mouth.

The tension fled. The judge visibly relaxed, a smile quirking up one corner of his mouth. "Yes. Next time you both can have friends over while Ms. Kay and I go out. Now hurry up and get ready for school."

After breakfast, the kids helped me load the puppies into the car and we all went our separate ways. Once Molly and I got the pups settled at the office, we both dove into work. The day flew by, and at five o'clock, I herded the pups back into my car and headed to see Grace.

As I drove to Prucilla's, I once again thought that although I'd miss these guys when they were gone, I'd also breathe a sigh of relief. Puppies were a huge responsibility, and carting them around, back and forth to work was really a pain.

At Prucilla's, I ended up locking them in the car, safely in their crates, with the windows cracked open a bit. It wasn't so cold that they'd be chilled, and I wanted them to have fresh air, even though I only intended on being inside for a few minutes.

Grace and her mother were both there. There were a bunch of boxes in the dining room, each holding clothes or various household goods.

"We're trying to sort through Aunt Pru's belongings." Grace ran a hand through her hair. "There's so much. Mom and I aren't sure what to keep, but these are the things we've decided absolutely can be donated."

"It takes time," I assured her. "My husband passed almost a year ago and I still have things of his I haven't been able to part with yet. Better to keep something and decide later, than to get rid of it and regret you let it go."

"That's what we're thinking. We're definitely keeping the dog show memorabilia. Mom's fixing the trophies that were broken. I hate that they were used in Aunt Pru's murder because she was so proud of them. I'd like to keep them, but I don't know if I can ever forget they were part of a crime scene."

Grace led me into the kitchen where an older version of herself was applying some industrial strength glue to the broken trophies scattered on a table.

I handed Grace eight folders. "Daisy has given her okay for all five of her pups—she interviewed the applicants and did a site visit on each of them. I did an interview and site visit for the family who wants to adopt Lacey. The other two of mine are people I know personally and can vouch for. I just need you to give me the thumbs-up, and that'll be eight puppies with wonderful forever homes."

"Which leaves only one," she said, taking the folders. "Do you have any pending applications for that pup?"

"No." Poor little Cagney. "I know there's the perfect family out there for her somewhere. She's so sweet. I'm sure it won't be long before she's in her forever home."

"I hope so. I really appreciate you and Daisy doing this for us, and for the rescue."

Grace took the folders to the kitchen island to peruse, while I went over and introduced myself to Grace's mother.

"Patricia," she told me, shaking my outstretched hand. "Grace told me all you and your friend have been doing to help out. Pru's dogs were everything to her. She'd be happy knowing those puppies were being taken care of and being provided for."

"It's no problem. And I'm sorry for your loss." I eyed the trophies. "Do you show dogs as well? I remember Grace mentioning you were at a show when she got the news."

She nodded. "I show Boxers, just like Pru did before she started devoting all of her time to the rescue and animal advocacy. We grew up competing in conformance shows. I also do obedience shows with mine. Boxers are smart dogs. Whew, the energy though. It's not a breed for the faint of heart, let me tell you."

"Maybe that's why Prucilla was switching to French Bull-dogs?" Although Gus seemed to be pretty lively, he was just a puppy. I couldn't see him ever being quite as energetic as a Boxer.

"How did you know Pru was looking into showing Frenchies?" Patricia's eyebrows went up.

"From a woman over in Lakepoint," I told her. "Prucilla had gone to see her a week or so ago about her grandfather's French Bulldogs and that bloodline." I frowned. "And I thought Grace had told me you'd said Prucilla was getting back into showing."

"I think she missed it," Patricia said. "She was very supportive of careful breeding. Said it was important that people who wanted pet dogs be able to find genetically healthy and temperamentally sound ones. If ethical breeders were vilified, that would mean the only alternative for buyers would be puppy mill dogs, and backyard breeders. Her passion was rescue, but she'd seen plenty of dogs with genetic abnormalities and health problems come through her door. She believed every one of those dogs deserved a loving home with proper medical care, but she felt the long-term solution was to encourage careful breeding and come down hard on puppy mills as well as abuse and neglect cases."

It sounded a lot like what Tommy Frys had espoused during our meeting, except he was not a fan of breeding.

"Education," Patricia continued, ticking each off on her fingers. "Free spay and neuter clinics. Free rabies and shot clinics. Free education and genetic screening for any dog owner who thought they might be interested in letting Spot have a litter of puppies. Funding for fosters and rescues to provide lifetime medical care for unadoptable dogs, and funding for shelters so no dog needed to be put down outside a clear quality of life issue."

"That's a lot to take on without adding in dog shows and possibly breeding," I commented.

"Which is why I think Prucilla was just talking out of nostalgia. She missed showing. Missed producing the best quality puppies. But I don't think she would have been willing to take time out from her rescue and advocacy to do that." Patricia snorted. "Frenchies. I don't understand why she wouldn't have gone back to Boxers."

I shrugged. "They *are* cute. My friend just got one. And Prucilla *did* go talk to Vicky Ellinger about her grandfather's Frenchies."

Patricia shot me a quick glance, then went back to gluing

the trophies. "Wilmont's Heart of a Lion? Pru and I talked about him. There haven't been any promising dogs out of that line for the last five years. The first six litters Denny Topper bred from Lion were amazing, but everything after that has been...meh. I told her if she wanted to get back into the show ring, she could do better. Denny Topper's charging a fortune for his pups, but I'm just not seeing them bringing home the trophies like they were a decade ago."

I thought of Olive's puppy and winced. "Really? The granddaughter said the genetics were strong, and the line bred true."

She shrugged. "It did breed true when Lion was alive. And like I said, the first six litters were incredible. I don't know what happened. Maybe Topper is using sub-par females? Who knows."

"Do you think the semen has degraded over time? It has been cryogenically frozen for ten years." I couldn't help but be suspicious that a technique that froze living cells wouldn't somehow adversely affect them.

"Oh no!" She chuckled. "It may sound sketchy, but that technique is solid. The lab tests each straw for viability. Once thawed, the existing sperm are just as genetically sound as fresh—there are just fewer of them sometimes. That's why when you're breeding with frozen samples, you occasionally have to use three or four straws. People breeding performance horses and even cattle use the same techniques. Back in the day I had a litter by a famous Boxer out of Germany, and the dog never got within a thousand miles of my kennel."

Ugh. I hoped that Olive hadn't spent a fortune on a dog that wasn't going to go anywhere in the show ring. Although from what she and Suzette had said, they were doing this more as a fun hobby than any desire to win big.

But competition was still competition, and I doubted Olive would have shelled out the big bucks for Gus if she hadn't had some expectation that he'd be a winner in the ring.

"All done. These puppies have my blessing to go to their new homes."

I turned to see Grace handing me the folders. "Thank you. I'll give you a call once I get things squared away with the remaining pup."

Knowing I needed to get back to the car and get the puppies home, I said my goodbyes, told Patricia that it had been nice meeting her, and headed outside.

Eight out of nine puppies adopted. I glanced in the rearview mirror at my four, eyeing the little brown one with the black mask who hadn't yet found a home. Cagney was so cute with her dark golden-colored fur and brown eyes that I knew we'd find the perfect home for her soon.

And if not, well, one puppy in the house would be a whole lot easier to handle than four. I wouldn't be sad if Cagney stayed a few more weeks. But if she did, I knew it would be even harder to let her go when she was finally adopted.

CHAPTER 22

I dropped off Daisy's folders with the applications for her puppies and gave her the go-ahead with Grace's approval. Then I headed home, for once arriving early enough to get dinner started.

With the puppies contained in the powder room and Taco outside making his evening rounds, I pulled the ground beef out of the fridge and started making mini-meatloaves. By the time the kids came through the door, the meatloaves were in the oven, green beans with ham bits were on the stove, and I was poking the baked potatoes to assess their doneness.

In between my dinner prep, I'd called Rachel, Miles, and Molly to let them know they were free to pick up their puppies anytime. It was going to be a bittersweet evening with the pups leaving for their new families, and meatloaf was my comfort food.

"Mmmm, meatloaf," Henry said as he peeked into the oven.

"Taco came in with us," Madison announced, as though I

197

couldn't see the cat circling his food bowl, meowing with impatience. "Should I feed him?"

"Yes, please. And the puppies, too. Make sure you give them lots of love, because they're going to their new homes tonight," I said to them both.

"Even Cagney?" There was a faint note of panic to Madison's voice that had me realizing I wasn't the only one who'd come to love these puppies.

"Cagney is staying for a little while longer," I told her. "Have you heard from your dad? I'm not sure if I should put dinner on the table or hold off."

"I'm here!" a voice called from the foyer. Seconds later the judge appeared, plopping his briefcase on a chair. "What help do you need, Kay?"

I handed him a stack of plates. "Can you set the table while Madison and Henry are feeding the four-legged crew?"

We sat down to dinner, chatting about our days as we always did. Our kiss hadn't seemed to have changed things between the judge and me. I was grateful, glad that we could continue such easy conversation around the kids, but I was also confused. Would we be kissing in secret, only when the kids weren't with us? Was Valentine's Day just a weird anomaly, and we'd never kiss again? I could still feel the pull of attraction between us, but I wasn't sure what the rules were in a game I hadn't played since I'd been in college.

After dinner, the judge took care of the dishes in order to give Madison and Henry time to play with the puppies. I pulled ingredients out of the cabinets to bake apple spice muffins for the morning. Our arms occasionally touched as we worked, and the judge brushed his hand along my back as he walked by to put the leftovers in the fridge. So affectionate touches only when the kids weren't present? At least for now?

Ugh, I was going to drive myself crazy trying to analyze

the nuances of every glance and every touch. We'd need to talk about this sort of thing soon, decide how we were going to present our budding romance to his kids and when. But not now.

The doorbell rang. I shoved the muffins in the oven, quickly set the timer, and ran to answer the door as the puppies barked excitedly from the powder room. A shadowy figured appeared in the hallway, startling me. Prucilla's ghost hadn't come to my house before, and I hadn't seen her spirit in days.

The ghost's appearance made sense when I opened the door. There stood Rachel with her two girls, here to pick up Lacey. Prucilla's spirit hovered, gliding forward to give what looked like her blessing to Lacey as Rachel picked the little puppy up. Soon after, Molly and Hunter came for Starsky, the ghost appearing once more to touch the pup as he left for his new home. The kids were starting on their homework when Violet and Miles came by to pick up Hutch.

"Congratulations," I said as I saw the ring on Violet's finger.

She smiled, radiating happiness. "Thank you!"

"What's this? A Valentine's Day engagement?" Judge Beck clapped Miles on the shoulder. "Good job, buddy. I wish you both a lifetime of happiness."

Miles grinned. "Thanks. I'm a lucky guy."

"I'm a lucky girl," Violet countered, putting her arm around Miles's waist.

"And here's the stork, bringing you your first baby," Henry said as he held Hutch out to Miles. "Are you going to change his name? Will you bring him by on Friday for happy hour so we can see him?"

As with the others, Prucilla's spirit appeared, brushing a ghostly hand along Hutch's head as Miles tucked the puppy against his chest.

"We've decided to keep the name Hutch," Miles said, absolutely unaware of the ghost that stood right beside him. "The name suits him. I might be working the late shift Friday, so it's up to Violet if she can bring him or not."

"I'll definitely bring him," Violet assured Henry. "It's going to be puppy central here, with Hutch and Gus."

"And Starsky," I told her. "Molly and her brother Harper adopted him, and they decided to keep the name as well. So Hutch will be reunited with his old partner during Friday happy hours."

"Too bad Olive didn't call Gus Huggy Bear," Judge Beck said. "I like consistent themes in my pet names."

"Dad. Taco?" Madison poked her father in the side. "I'm pretty sure there's no Taco in that Starsky and Hutch show."

"Taco is the bad guy who steals the puppy food and pukes in the hallway," I told her.

"I doubt either Starsky or Hutch will have the nerve to arrest your cat." Violet laughed.

"We better get going," Miles told her. "We need to unpack, then I need to get Hutch situated before I head off to work."

We saw them off, the ghost vanishing as the couple left with Starsky. I turned to see Madison cuddling Cagney. Her eyes shone wet with unshed tears, and her mouth wobbled slightly before she buried her face in the puppy's fur.

I knew exactly how she felt.

Judge Beck sighed. "Go ahead and take her upstairs when you do your homework, but she's not sleeping in your bed, okay?"

Madison smiled at her father over top of the puppy's head. "Thanks, Dad."

"Can Cagney sleep in *my* room?" Henry asked as his sister ran upstairs.

"No, but you can do homework with her tomorrow

night." The judge shot me a quick glance. "If she's still here, that is."

"She'll still be here," I told Henry. There were no applications for little Cagney yet. Just the reminder of that hurt my heart.

Henry headed upstairs to do his homework while the judge and I spread our laptops and files across the dining room table, settling in as we did most nights to catch up on our own work. We sat in companionable silence; the judge getting up at one point and returning with two mugs of herbal tea. At nine o'clock, the kids came down to wish us goodnight. I didn't have the heart to leave Cagney in the powder room all by herself, so I set her on my lap. She snuggled in and fell asleep, her warm, furry chest rising and falling rhythmically with each breath.

I'd finished my work for the evening, but wasn't ready to go up yet, so I sipped tea, stroked a sleeping Cagney, and thought about Prucilla's murder. I wondered if Detective Keeler was any closer to finding the killer? I certainly wasn't. In fact, I was totally out of suspects at this point.

"Penny for your thoughts." Judge Beck shut his laptop lid and leaned his elbows on the table.

"I was hoping the detective had more leads on Prucilla's murder than I do," I told him. "I stopped by her house this afternoon to get Grace to sign off on the puppy adoptions. She and her mother were going through Prucilla's things. Patricia, Prucilla's sister, was trying to glue the broken dog show trophies back together. Both women said they'd meant a lot to Prucilla."

"It wasn't just a fun, competitive hobby to her," the judge mused. "She must have had great pride in working to improve the breed, and in providing people with the highest quality puppies."

I dug my fingers into Cagney's fur. "This right here is the

highest quality puppy, in my opinion. But I get it. I really do
My thoughts went to Olive and Gus. "Patricia told me some
thing that really bothered me. She said her sister had talke
to her about French Bulldogs, and was asking about puppie
from that Denny Topper guy—the one Olive got Gus from
Patricia said that in spite of their famous lineage, none o
those puppies he's been selling are all that great."

"Sour grapes?" Judge Beck shrugged. "They're kind o
competitors, even though they're not showing the sam
breed. Maybe she's jealous that his puppies are from som
big-name Westminster show winner."

I frowned. "I didn't get that sort of vibe from her at all. Plu
she and her sister were close. If Prucilla wanted to show
different breed, then I think Patricia would have wanted t
steer her to the best breeder, the best litters of puppies. She tol
me the first six litters that Denny Topper sold were exemplary
but that all the puppies since then were no more than average."

"And you're worried that Olive might have bee
scammed?" Judge Beck asked.

"Not scammed, but maybe misled?" I chewed on my li
and thought a bit. "I'm sure she did her research, but sh
hasn't been showing for years, where Patricia is very activ
in showing her Boxers. Maybe this is the sort of thing tha
gets whispered around the show ring, but isn't widel
known."

"People wouldn't want to talk bad about another kenne
or breeder," the judge agreed. "It would be bad form."

"I just hate the thought that Olive may have spent a lot o
money for a puppy that isn't going to be bringing home th
trophies."

Judge Beck slid his laptop into his briefcase and began t
pack up his folders. "There are no guarantees that *any* pupp
is going to grow up into the sort of dog that wins big a

shows. She bought a good pup from a good breeder with an excellent lineage. The rest is up to chance."

I closed my laptop and began to gather my paperwork as well. "I know. It's just that this guy is trading on that Lion dog's famous name. Patricia said maybe he's been breeding to sub-par females or something."

"Why would he do that?" The judge stood. "That famous Lion dog is long dead. He's only got so many straws of frozen semen before he runs out and it's gone forever. It's in his best interest to use it wisely, not go wasting it on what Patricia thinks are sub-par females."

"You're right." And I was going to keep my mouth shut about this whole thing. I didn't want Olive to have doubts about her puppy, or the breeder she'd researched so carefully. And whether Gus brought home the trophies or not, he was still adorable. And his lineage was still impressive. Hadn't Olive said there were only one hundred and twenty pups sired by Lion in the last ten years—since Denny Topper had bought the straws of frozen semen from Gus Wilmont's estate?

"I'm heading up." Judge Beck hesitated, then leaned forward to plant a quick kiss on my lips. "I really did enjoy last night. Maybe this weekend, we can watch that movie and eat my popcorn?"

And do other things? Goodness, I hoped so.

"Friday night after the porch happy hour? Or maybe Saturday night?" I remembered that the kids would be here this weekend. "Or Sunday after Madison and Henry go to Heather's?"

"Friday night. I'm not patient enough to wait until Sunday for my movie and popcorn."

"Me either," I said, knowing we were talking about more than just movies and popcorn.

"Then it's a date." He picked up his briefcase and set it aside. "Goodnight, Kay. Don't stay up too late."

"I won't," I promised, watching him leave. I listened to his footsteps on the stairs, then sat alone at the dining room table for a while, stroking Cagney's soft fur.

One hundred and twenty puppies. I frowned, opening my laptop back up and Googling the average litter size for French Bulldogs. Three. Three pups per litter, and that was an optimistic number.

The fakes are never as good as the real thing. The judge had said that about purses, but did that apply to other things as well? Patricia had said the first six litters from Lion's frozen semen straws had been amazing, but other litters hadn't been.

Some of the swimmers died with frozen semen. The lab tested motility, sending multiple straws out to ensure a litter of puppies actually occurred.

I did the math. Three straws per insemination. Six litters. That was eighteen straws.

Vicky had said the estate sold twenty-four straws. That would be eight litters. But Olive had said there were one hundred and twenty pups reputed to have been sired by Lion after his owner's death. That would have required roughly one hundred and fifty straws. There hadn't been one hundred and fifty straws. There hadn't even been fifty straws.

I played around with the numbers. If every single straw was chock full of swimmers, and each litter was an average of five pups, then the numbers worked out to one hundred and twenty. But that just wasn't possible. French Bulldogs didn't have litters that big—maybe one might as a fluke, but not five every single litter, and certainly not an average. And I was pretty sure the best cryogenic facility in the world wouldn't be able to thaw out twenty-four straws with one hundred percent motility in each one.

It just didn't make sense. Maybe Vicky had been wrong about the number of straws in the estate. Maybe there were forty-two straws and not twenty-four. Maybe Olive had been mistaken about the report and it hadn't been one hundred and twenty puppies sired by Lion once Denny Topper bought the frozen semen from the estate. Maybe some of those had been grandpups.

There had to be a reasonable explanation for this, because I didn't want to think that my friend had been taken in as part of some dog-breeding scam. I'd make a few phone calls tomorrow and straighten this all out. There clearly was a mistake somewhere—a reasonable explanation for this.

I picked up Cagney and stood. Then I took her upstairs to sleep the night in my bedroom, because the no non-house-broken dogs in bedrooms rule the judge had talked about clearly did not apply to me.

CHAPTER 23

*D*aisy's and my morning yoga was a bit more subdued with only Lady and Cagney racing around the yard. Afterward we sat outside, bundled up in blankets, as we drank our coffee, ate apple spice muffins, and watched the dogs play. I fed Taco and Cagney, putting the pup in the powder room to eat, then went upstairs to shower and get ready for work.

Even the ride in to the office was less stressful, with only one puppy whining and barking in the back seat as opposed to four. Cagney was less rowdy without her siblings to spur her on, and she quickly settled down underneath my desk with a few toys and a chew to gnaw on. Molly, J.T., and I slid back into our usual routine without the chaos of the last few days.

I took Cagney for a walk at lunchtime, picking up a sandwich at the corner deli and eating it on the go. As we strolled, my thoughts kept returning to that French Bulldog breeder, and the impossible number of puppies he'd managed to get out of only twenty-four straws of frozen semen.

Back at the office, I picked up the phone and called Vicky Ellinger.

"It's Kay Carrera, the private investigator that spoke to you yesterday about Prucilla Downing and her visit to you." I took out my notepad as I spoke. "I'm so sorry to bother you, but do you know the name of the facility where your grand-father stored Lion's semen?"

"Wheelhouse Biostorage. Why?"

"You're positive there were only twenty-four straws of semen when they were sold?" I asked.

"Yes. We needed to value them per straw for the estate. I remember, thinking it was a shame Grandpa hadn't stored more. Why?"

"There are too many pups," I told her. "I read that the average litter for a French Bulldog is three. Is that right?"

She laughed. "If you're lucky. There are cases of litters as large as seven, but that's incredibly rare. Usually it's two or three. Maybe four. My Goldens tend to have eight, but Frenchies generally have small litters."

"And how many straws does it usually take per litter?" I asked.

"Three is common." She paused for a second. "Two or three, I'd say. Using only one leaves a huge risk that the preg-nancy won't take, and you'll have wasted a straw. It's better to spend the extra and get two, because there's always some motility loss in the freezing and thawing process. Best to get three. If you're going to all that trouble and expense, you don't want to cheap out and not end up with any puppies at all."

I did some quick math on my pad of paper. "So, let's say there are four pups in a litter, and the breeder only used one straw per pregnancy. That's ninety-six puppies—an incred-ibly optimistic ninety-six puppies."

"More likely it would be three pups per litter with two

straws per breeding," Vicky countered. "That's still optimistic, but it could happen."

"That's thirty-six puppies," I told her. "There should only be thirty-six puppies registered after your grandfather's death with Lion as the sire. My friend has a paper from the AKC that says there have been one hundred and twenty."

Vicky sucked in a breath. "That...that can't be right. Are you sure that doesn't include grandpups? Or maybe that includes *all* pups sired by Lion, even those that occurred during his lifetime? But even that wouldn't make sense. My grandfather was very picky about who he bred Lion to. I doubt there were more than twenty puppies in his lifetime that Lion had sired."

"So, fifty-six in total." I scribbled the number on my pad of paper. "Let's round it up and say sixty. That's still not close to the one hundred and twenty the AKC report says, even if my friend misspoke and that number was a grand total and not just since Fairwoods Kennel and Denny Topper started breeding using Lion as a sire."

"There must be some mistake," Vicky insisted. "I know there were only twenty-four straws. I'm positive on that number. It was part of the estate accounting, and I remember wishing that my grandfather had banked more, because Lion was such an amazing dog."

"Have you been following any of the puppies from Lion's line?" I asked her. "I know you show Golden Retrievers and that's not even the same group, but I wondered if you noticed any big wins lately from the Fairwoods Kennel pups."

"The first year or two I did," she said. "I remember being proud that Lion was still producing such great puppies, but I don't think I've seen many over the last five or so years. It's not surprising. I mean, there were only twenty-four straws. I assumed Denny Topper had already used them all, or maybe was holding some back for a very special litter. With only twenty-four straws, I wouldn't have expected to see show rings filled with Lion's puppies."

I wondered how many litters Denny Topper had attributed to Lion? Clearly a lot if the AKC showed one hundred twenty pups sired by the dog.

"I'm trying to come up with a reasonable explanation for this. The cryogenic facility couldn't have screwed things up, could they?" I asked. "Maybe they stored some other dog's semen next to Lion's, and it got comingled?"

"That's not possible," she said firmly. "First, Denny Topper knew there were only twenty-four straws. If the facility kept sending him more, then he would have known something was wrong. Secondly, the way they're stored doesn't allow for comingling of samples. There are containers stored in containers, and they're all bar coded and scanned in. Besides, if Denny Topper had been using another dog's semen, the puppies would have looked mixed breed."

"So the facility couldn't have screwed up, and you're positive there were only twenty-four straws…" I mused.

"I'm *positive*. It was in the estate reckoning. And if you doubt me, you can check with the facility. I'll sign off on it. Grandpa had both my mother and me as authorized users, and even though we sold the straws, there was a contract where we could continue to receive data and records." She made a huffing sound. "Not that we would have any reason to bother. Mother was no longer showing at that point, and I'm breeding Goldens. As far as I was concerned, sold was sold, but Grandpa was paranoid and had all sorts of stuff built into the contract."

"Thanks. I might need that authorization in the future," I told her.

"Anytime." She let out a long breath. "If Denny Topper is ripping people off, falsifying that litters are being sired by Lion when they're not, then he needs to be named and shamed in the dog show and breeding community. People should sue, recover damages. I'm just so angry thinking that someone might have done something like that. Lion was my grandfather's legacy. We do what we do to improve the breeds we love. Lying, cheating, trading on Lion's name for profit...that's a crime."

I agreed. But as I hung up with Vicky, I wondered what the heck I was going to do about it.

"Can I run something by you?" I asked Molly.

She swiveled her chair around, eyeing me with surprise. "Me? Sure."

"This is confidential," I told her.

She made a zipped-lips motion.

"That cute puppy Olive just got?" I waited for her to nod. "I think the breeder is running a scam. He's claiming the sire of these pups is that famous French Bulldog, but I think that's a lie. I think he's using another dog to sire these litters and claiming it's the famous one. That semen should have been used up years ago based on the numbers, but he's still registering pups as being sired through that line."

She frowned. "Could he do that without getting caught?"

I nodded. "Easily. Remember Olive said that famous dog died ten years ago, and that the breeder is using the frozen semen he purchased when the dog's owner passed? From what I gather, it's kind of an honor system when registering the pedigree of the litters. The breeder is certifying this particular dog sired the litter, but unless someone goes through the expense of running the DNA, it's all based on the breeder's word."

"If someone lied and got caught, would they be shunned in the community or something?" she asked. "Not allowed to compete in shows?"

"I think so. And they'd possibly face civil litigation," I added. "No one had cause to check into any of this. Even famous dogs sometimes have litters that aren't all that amazing. So if your dog with the impressive pedigree doesn't wind up winning big...well, these things happen."

"And I'll bet the cryogenic facility wouldn't release information to non-owners about how many vials or whatever are left," Molly mused. "So the breeder could lie and unless someone paid a ton of money and took a chance on a lawsuit to gain the information, no one would know."

"Except the granddaughter of the famous dog's owner knows exactly how many samples were sold as part of the estate. It's documented. And the numbers don't add up with the AKC paperwork of how many pups are reported as being sired by the famous dog. And the granddaughter has a legal right to know how many semen straws are still at the storage facility."

"Wow, this is serious stuff." Molly stood and began to pace. "Olive could sue. Lots of people could sue."

"But I'm not sure I should tell her." I looked over at Cagney, snoozing beside J.T.'s desk. "She'll still keep Gus. She'll still show him. Would she want to know that her puppy isn't what she thought he was? That the breeder lied? That she paid way too much for a dog that was supposed to have this famous pedigree, and now doesn't?"

Molly stopped pacing. "I...I don't know. I'm not sure I'd want to know, but I'm not interested in dog shows or any of that. If she'd bought Gus just as a pet, then maybe it would be better if she didn't know. But she's going to show him. And what if she decides to breed him? Then it's not just Olive this guy lied to. That lie is going to be passed on to the people who'd buy puppies sired by Gus."

"You're right. She deserves to know." I hoped Olive and I were still friends after this. Some people didn't take kindly to hearing bad news, and some people blamed the messenger. I didn't think Olive was like that, but I hadn't known her for very long, and I didn't want to lose a friendship over this.

"Maybe she can get some money back from the breeder," Molly suggested. "Gus is still a pedigree dog, still registered. She can show him and love him, but she shouldn't have paid that much for him."

I thought through that, then shook my head. "The only way I can see that happening is if Olive signed some sort of non-disclosure, and Olive wouldn't do that. She'd burst in there, demand her money back, then tell that man she was going to let every single person on that AKC list know that he was a cheat and a liar."

I envisioned that encounter in my mind, seeing Olive confronting the breeder and not backing down. It would get ugly.

It would get more than ugly.

"Oh no!" I stared at Molly in horror. "I think...I think I know who killed Prucilla Downing."

Her eyebrows went up. "Who? And what...the lying breeder?"

"I've got no proof," I told her. "But Prucilla Downing was asking the famous dog's granddaughter about the breeder, and she'd talked to her sister about it. She knows pedigree dog breeding, knows dog shows. She would have run the numbers just like I did, and known what the breeder was doing. Prucilla had a history of not backing down from a confrontation."

"You really think that breeder would have killed her?" Molly asked.

"Hear me out." It was my turn to stand and start pacing. "Wednesday, Prucilla meets with Vicky Ellinger about her grandfather's estate and the semen straws, and Denny Topper's kennel. She talks to her sister. She probably gets the same AKC report that Olive got. She runs the numbers, and knows that Denny Topper is defrauding people."

"So why not report him?" Molly asked. "Tell the AKC. Tell the people who bought pups from him."

"That's not her style," I guessed, thinking that wouldn't be most people's style. "Sneaking behind someone's back and reporting him? No, Prucilla would have met with Denny Topper and accused him to his face."

"But why would she let him in her house?" Molly asked. "If she'd confronted him, and they'd had a fight, then this Denny Topper drove to Prucilla's house, she wouldn't have let him in."

"I think she hadn't had the confrontation *until* she let him in," I conjectured. "She called him, said she wanted to talk to him about buying a puppy, or maybe partnering on a Frenchie rescue or something. Then after he's there, in her house, she accused him of defrauding people." I stopped my pacing and faced Molly. "It's Prucilla's house. She's confident there. She feels safe there. She'd never expect Denny Topper to get angry enough to kill her with one of her own trophies."

Molly frowned. "That's a lot of speculation, Kay."

"I know. There's not enough evidence to accuse the guy of murder, but the shop that sold the fur said a man bought it. The clerk said she'd recognize him. If she identified Denny Topper as the buyer of that coyote fur coat that was found slashed up at the scene of the murder, that might be enough for Detective Keeler to bring him in."

"It's still not enough to charge him with murder," Molly said, her voice full of doubt.

"It's not," I agreed. "But it's a start."

"So…are you going to tell Olive?" she asked.

I sighed, looking over at the sleeping Cagney. "Yes, I'm going to tell Olive."

CHAPTER 24

I held the phone away from my ear as Olive called Denny Topper some rather choice names.

"Are you sure there were only twenty-four straws when he bought them?" Olive asked.

"The granddaughter is positive. She said it's on the estate paperwork, so it's easy to prove. The county will have a copy of it, and she does as well. Plus, after she got off the phone with me she called the cryogenic facility, and they told her that the last of Lion's straws had been sent out almost five years ago."

Vickie had called me right before I'd picked up the phone to call Olive. She'd been furious. I wasn't sure who was going to beat the stuffing out of Denny Topper first, my friend, or Gus Wilmont's granddaughter.

"They don't keep for years once they're thawed out, so right there that's proof that he lied on Gus's pedigree. He lied about all the pups in that litter and probably a dozen other litters," Olive snapped.

"At least that many." I sighed. "Olive, I'm so sorry. I really didn't want to tell you this, but I thought you needed to know."

"I'm glad you told me. I love Gus, and I'm keeping him no matter what, but I'm getting my money back from Denny Topper if I have to turn him upside down and shake it out of him."

Olive had double-checked the report she'd gotten from the AKC, but at this point it didn't matter whether the one hundred twenty puppies were truly registered as sired by Lion or his grandpups. There hadn't been any semen straws left to use for nearly five years.

It might not matter in Olive's case, but it would certainly matter for the people who had purchased the puppies on that report, though.

"I'm leaving work and I'm going over there right now," Olive vowed.

"No!" I thought of Prucilla, dead on her living room floor, and didn't want to take the chance that my friend might meet the same fate. "You can't just go over there and accuse him. Call a lawyer or something, and just sue."

"Not until I look that man in the face and give him a piece of my mind. I want to hear what he's got to say for himself. Then I'll talk to a lawyer."

"You can't go there alone, Olive." I got up and grabbed my coat off the back of my chair. "I'm coming too. I'll meet you there. Do not go in without me, okay? Promise me, Olive."

I hurriedly asked Molly to watch Cagney, told her to call Detective Keeler and tell him my suspicions, no matter how crazy he might think me, then raced out the door. Googling the address, I sped through town and managed to pull in the drive just behind Olive's car. We both parked, and I had to rush to get out of my car, jogging to keep up with a furious Olive.

Like Vicky Ellinger's business, Denny Topper was

running a boarding kennel, complete with grooming services and dog enrichment activities. He also provided dog training with group classes announced to start this Friday as per a sign by the driveway entrance. Fairview Kennels was also a farm, complete with six horses grazing in a field, and a handful of goats in a fenced in area.

Olive stomped up to the boarding business entrance and flung the door open.

"Where's Denny Topper?" she demanded to a startled young woman.

"At the house. Can I help you?" The woman's eyes were wide, her gaze darting to the exit.

"You can get him. Tell him Olive O'Toole is here to see him."

"Umm. Okay." Instead of picking up the phone, the woman rounded the counter and went out the door, sprinting toward the house.

I took the opportunity to look around. It was a small room with an l-shaped counter in the center. Behind the counter were shelves holding dog shampoo, bags of dog treats, and six large trophies. Dozens of dog show pictures and award plaques were lined up on the rear wall along with a rack of dog leashes. There was a door to the right of the counter. I went to the door and peeked through the window before swinging it open to better see the kennel area. There were two lines of neat kennels with doors connecting each to an outdoor run. Three kennels had pairs of black and tan French Bulldogs, all eyeing me curiously in between barks. Another kennel held a Labrador Retriever, and another some sort of hound. The place was immaculate and well cared for, but I immediately contrasted it with Vicky's busy, and probably more successful business.

Olive grumbled and paced until we finally saw the woman and a man walking with casual slowness from the house. The man looked to be in his fifties, average height, maybe a little on the short side with thinning dark hair. Not attractive, but not unattractive either. Midway to the kennel office, Denny paused, said something to the woman, then continued on as she turned back for the house.

He smiled as he came in, the smile not quite reaching his eyes. "Ms. O'Toole. What can I do for you? Is something the matter with Gus?"

"Gus is fine, but something is the matter with his pedigree," Olive snapped. "He's not what you represented. There's no way Wilmont's Heart of a Lion sired him. The cryogenic facility says the last of Lion's semen straws were sent out five years ago."

Denny Topper's smile and calm demeanor remained unchanged. "That's because I had them moved to another facility for easier access five years ago.

Olive faltered at that, but I stepped forward. "There were only twenty-four straws of Lion's semen at the time of Gus Wilmont's death. That's how many were sold to you as part of the estate. Olive has a report from the AKC that says you somehow managed to get one hundred and twenty pups out of that with an average litter size of three for French Bulldogs? Even if you somehow managed to get a successful litter with only one straw every time, the numbers don't add up."

The man's smile tightened, but his voice still remained velvety smooth. "I don't know where you got that information, but it's wrong. The AKC must have sent you the wrong report, and I bought a lot more than twenty-four straws of Lion's semen. Clearly his granddaughter is mistaken. She was very young when her grandfather died, and her late mother took care of the estate. She must have misunderstood."

I believed Vicky. She was confident about the number of straws that were sold. Proving that would be easy with a few quick phone calls to the cryogenic facility and to the Registrar of Wills for the estate accounting. And it would be easy to verify that AKC report as well. Denny Topper was lying. All it would take is some investigation, and those lies would all unravel.

But the one thing that had struck me most was that Denny had known this information came from Vicky. I'd never mentioned that I spoke to Gus Wilmont's granddaughter. Clearly he'd had this argument with someone before—and I was pretty sure that someone was Prucilla Downing.

He'd killed her. I just knew it, but there was no concrete proof right now.

"I'm not a fool," Olive snapped. "I specifically ordered that report. It'll be easy for me to verify the how many of Lion's semen straws you bought from the estate. You defrauded me, Denny Topper. Fraud."

He held his hands out wide. "I promise that I did not defraud you. The AKC makes errors sometimes when putting together reports. All of this is just a big misunderstanding, but I want my customers to be happy. How about I refund you half of what you paid for your puppy, as a gesture of goodwill?"

Olive hesitated, and I knew she was wondering if she had the time to dig all this information up, the time to deal with a civil lawsuit, and the money to fight Denny Topper in court. And after all that, she might find out she'd been wrong, that the report had been wrong, or that Vicky had been wrong about the number of semen straws. She loved her dog. Yes, she was competitive, but she and Suzette were still showing as just a fun hobby.

What if Denny Topper was on the level? I had a habit of jumping to conclusions. Usually I was right, but what if this time I wasn't? I'd let Olive do whatever she decided was right, then I'd go back to the office and dig until I was satisfied. I'd get a copy of the estate accounting. I'd get another report from the AKC. I'd get Vicky to approve a statement from the cryogenic facility about the inventory of Lion's samples—how many had been there when Denny bought them, and exactly when and how many had been disbursed over the years?

I'd dig further. Then if Olive or the other purchasers of puppies wanted to take action, they could. And if I found out that I'd been mistaken? I'd swallow my pride and apologize to both my friend and this man whose smug smile I absolutely hated.

"You'll still have an amazing, show-quality pup at a ridiculously low price," Denny continued. "And he still has Lion's name on his pedigree. That alone is of value, even if he ends up not doing as well in the show ring as you'd hoped. You can breed him, and people will pay top dollar for one of Lion's grandpups."

"I don't care about making money off breeding him," Olive replied. "I just don't like thinking that I was lied to and ripped off."

"You weren't." Denny's voice was soft and reassuring. He moved behind the desk and pulled a lockbox out from under the counter. "I'll refund you half of what you paid for Gus, though. Just because I want you to be happy—with him and with me."

When he set the lockbox on the counter, I noticed a healing wound on his hand. It looked like a bite mark, and I immediately thought back to Lady and the day of Prucilla's murder. Had Lady bit the killer? The wound on Denny Topper's hand looked a lot like a bite mark, but he worked with dogs every day, and had a few borders back in the kennel area. Having a dog bite on his hand could be easily explained.

I'd been wrong about Ken Wollitt. I could just as easily be wrong about this man as well.

A shadowy form materialized to my left where the wall of dog-show pictures was. One of them slid slightly askew—a posed picture of Denny Topper with several French Bull-dogs, all of them seated on a fur rug before a lit fireplace. The picture shifted back to center, then the shadow moved through the swinging door into the kennel.

As Denny and Olive continued to speak, I made my way to the wall. A few of the others were posed pictures of dogs or dogs and Denny. Others were Denny accepting a trophy or award from a neatly dressed man or woman, the canine winner standing on a round, raised dais between or beside them. Kneeling down, I looked at a small photo near the bottom right where a fur coat wearing Denny was posing with three dogs.

Okay, Denny Topper wears furs. I'd never known any man who'd done so, but according to the woman at the consignment shop, some guys did. When I got back, I'd definitely talk to Detective Keeler about my suspicions and suggest that the woman at the consignment shop might be able to identify the buyer of the fur coat in a lineup—and that the lineup should include Denny Topper.

That uneasy feeling returned. We shouldn't be here. The guy was a scumbag, and probably a murderer. I hadn't wanted Olive to come by herself, but we needed to leave.

I turned around to suggest she accept Denny's offer, just to get us out of here, and found my friend shaking her head.

"No. I can't," she told the man. "If you've defrauded me, then you've defrauded a whole lot of other people. I'm going to talk to a lawyer, and get the documents proving what you've done. People need to know that you're a cheat and a liar. I'm not going to take what I feel is hush money, and let you go on continuing to rip people off."

Denny Topper sighed. Then he pulled a gun out of the cash box and pointed it at Olive. Both of us raised our hands. I eyed the exit, but there was no way I could make it across the room without either me, or Olive, getting shot.

"That's something I can't let you do. I've worked too hard building my reputation to have you ruin it, and ruin me financially." He waved the gun toward the swinging door. "Both of you get back in the kennel area. It'll be easier to clean up than out here."

We were not going into the kennel area and coming out alive. But what could I do? I had nothing handy to throw at the man, and wasn't sure that would be a good plan when he had a gun pointed at Olive. Could I distract him in time for at least Olive to get away? Or keep him talking and hope that *someone* showed up to help us? The last time I'd been at this end of a gun, J.T. had come through the office door to save me. But J.T. didn't even know I was here, and I wasn't sure Molly had been able to get a hold of Detective Keeler—or that he'd think my wild conjectures enough proof for him to drop everything and drive out here.

Stalling by keeping the villain talking always worked in books and the movies, and it was the only option I could think of, so that's what I went with.

"You killed Prucilla," I blurted out. "She found out you were lying and defrauding people, and was going to expose you."

The pistol swiveled to point at me. Olive edged toward the door, but he saw the movement and jerked the gun back toward her.

"I didn't mean to kill her. I went there thinking she was interested in buying a puppy and getting back into dog shows. When she said..." Denny waved the gun wildly. "She threatened me. It was her own fault. She threatened me, so I hit her. I didn't plan on killing her."

I held my breath for a second, nearly peeing my pants at his carelessness with the gun. But Olive's and my lives were on the line. This was no time for panic. I needed to keep stalling until I could think of a way out of this, or until a miracle brought someone here just in time to save us.

"But you *did* kill her." I tried to steady my voice. "Then you broke the trophies, set the puppies and Lady free, and cut up your fur coat to try to cover it up."

"I liked that coat, but it was covered in blood. I figured if I cut it up and threw it on the floor with the broken trophies, the cops would think that Free the Fur nutjob had done it. I was going to do more, but someone was knocking on the door and coming in and I had to run." He glanced at his hand. "That stupid dog bit me. It was freezing cold without my coat and I had to walk two blocks and double back to get my car. I'm glad I didn't park in her driveway or I really would have been screwed."

"You're screwed anyway." It was time to lie a little. "The place where you bought the fur has your name on the receipt and your face on the security camera. Plus the clerk remembers you enough to pick you out in a lineup. You left blood at the scene from where Lady bit you. Fingerprints as well. I called Detective Keeler before we came out. He's on his way. Your best bet is to call a lawyer and claim self-defense or something, which you won't be able to do if you kill the two of us."

"Facing one murder charge is better than three," Olive told him. "And like you said, it was her fault. She threatened you. I'm sure your lawyer can cut a deal."

He seemed to think about that for a second, then his expression hardened and his finger moved to the trigger. "Either way I'm ruined."

Just then the swinging door to the kennel burst open, a shadowy figure preceding the dogs racing into the room.

Denny shifted his focus to the dogs and Olive dove forward, grabbing the man's wrist with both hands.

"Run," she shouted at me.

I didn't run. Instead I grabbed one of the trophies off the shelf and smashed Denny Topper in the back of the head with it. He swayed to the side, and threw out a hand for balance, his grip on the pistol loosening enough for Olive to wrestle it free.

With a far steadier aim than I would have had, my friend pointed the gun at our attacker, ordering him to keep his hands where we could see them. With dogs racing between our feet, I grabbed a handful of nylon leashes from a rack by the kennel door, and tied both Denny Topper's hands and feet.

Then I called the police.

CHAPTER 25

"*R*ed? Or white?" Judge Beck held up the bottles for me to pick.

"Both." This week's porch happy hour was a celebration. Denny Topper was in police custody, charged with murder, and Olive and I were alive.

That wasn't all we were celebrating. Eight of nine puppies had been adopted. Vicky Ellinger had gone public with Denny Topper's fraud, and in addition to criminal charges, he was facing a host of civil suits. Miles had gossiped that the man's fingerprints matched those he clearly hadn't had time to completely wipe off the murder weapon, and that he was positive some of the blood found at the scene would match his as well. Added to that, the woman at the consignment shop had called me Thursday evening, confirming that Denny Topper was the one who'd purchased the coyote fur coat. I'd passed the information along to Detective Keeler. It was more evidence for the murder trial, and I was happy to see one more nail in Denny Topper's coffin.

There would be lots of four-legged friends at today's

happy hour as well. Taco, already claiming his place of honor on the rocking chair. Daisy's Lady. Olive and Suzette with Gus. Molly and Hunter with Starsky. Violet and Miles with Hutch.

And Cagney. I looked down at the little brown puppy with her black markings. We'd had a few people express interest in her, but nothing had worked out, and I knew the longer she stayed with me, the harder it would be to let her go.

Judge Beck followed my gaze. "Heather called me this afternoon, asking if she could possibly take Cagney on a trial basis for a few months. The kids have been pestering her to keep the puppy, but she's worried she won't be able to handle having a dog by herself when Madison and Henry are here."

I bent down to scratch the pup behind her ears, then stood. "I don't know. I hate for her to be bounced around like that. What if Heather decides to keep her, only to realize in a few months that she can't handle having a dog? Cagney needs a forever home, not a maybe home."

The judge put the wine bottles on the counter and walked toward me. His arms came around my waist, pulling my back against him. "We could keep her ourselves."

His warm breath stirred a whole lot more than the hair near my ear, but I put a lid on those feelings. We had guests arriving soon. Plus the kids were here, and liable to burst into the kitchen at any moment.

"But can we handle a dog?" I asked. "I've been taking her to work each day, and she seems pretty chill without her brothers and sister racing around, but I really can't keep bringing her to the office. It's not fair to Molly, or to me, and I don't think an office dog is something J.T. will put up with long-term."

"People go to work and leave their dogs at home all the

time. Taco is here to keep Cagney company, and they seem to get along. We can crate her for safety while we're at work. You've got a fenced-in backyard for her to romp in. The kids can help walk her and take care of her while they're here."

I didn't want to be the one saying no to a dog when it had clearly been a sore spot between him and Heather, but I knew how much work a pet could be. There was a reason I'd come home from the shelter a year ago with a cat instead of a dog.

"She'd be your dog, not mine," I told him. "You're the one who needs to walk her, take her to vet appointments, arrange for boarding if we're going on vacation."

He was silent for a moment, then sighed. "You're right. A puppy is a lot of work, and a dog is a lifelong commitment. I should probably think about it some more before making a decision."

I turned in his arms, putting my palms on his chest. "Why don't we go ahead and let Heather take her for a few months. If Heather says no, we'll keep Cagney ourselves. That way she won't be bouncing around to a bunch of different houses. Either Heather adopts her, or we will."

He smiled down at me, settling his arms higher on my waist. "If she adopts Cagney, maybe we can still have the pup every other weekend."

I laughed. "Dog custody agreements?"

"It happens more than you'd think." He pulled me against him and kissed the side of my head.

Crazy as it sounded, this might be the best solution. We could dog-sit for Heather when she needed, and have designated visit times with Cagney when the kids were with us. And if Heather decided after a two-month trial that a puppy was too much for her, then we'd bring Cagney home.

"Okay. Go ahead and text Heather and let her know. Go ahead and tell the kids as well."

"Tell us what?" Madison burst through the kitchen door just as I'd feared. Instead of looking shocked at her father and me wrapped in each other's arms, she smirked and grabbed a cookie off the plate.

"Your mom is going to keep Cagney for a few months as a sort of dog-owner trial run." The judge removed one hand from my waist to hold up a finger before Madison could say anything. "Do not pressure her. She needs to make her own decision about this. You and Henry are going to both be out of the house in a few years, and she needs to be sure she really wants a dog. Got it?"

Madison nodded, picking up the plate. "Got it. And Dad?"

"Yes?" He returned both hands to my waist.

"You and Miss Kay are cute." With a saucy grin, the girl spun around and took the plates out to the porch.

"We're cute," I repeated to the judge.

He pulled away just enough to see my face, then he leaned down and placed a soft kiss on my lips. "Yes. We are cute. Now let's get this wine out there before our friends and their canine menageries arrive. We can continue being cute later tonight when the kids are in bed and we're watching a movie and eating buffalo-spice popcorn, or whatever is in that giant tin you bought me."

That giddy, happy feeling swept through me again, and I smiled up at him. "It's a date."

Pulling apart, we each grabbed a bottle of wine, then headed out to the porch, where I could already hear happy voices in conversation, punctuated by the occasional bark of a dog.

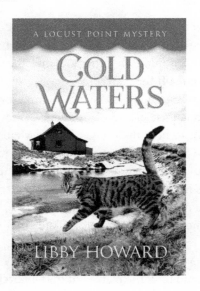

WANT to read more about Kay and her friends? Cold Waters, book 12 in the Locust Point Mystery Series, will be released this fall. To keep up with new releases, recipes and more, sign up for my newsletter HERE.

ACKNOWLEDGMENTS

Thanks to Lyndsey Lewellen for cover design and typography, and to Kim Cannon for copyediting. And special thanks to all my readers who love Kay and her friends. Read, bake, snuggle your Taco, and take a chance on love.

ABOUT THE AUTHOR

Libby Howard lives in a little house in the woods with her sons and two exuberant bloodhounds. She occasionally knits, occasionally bakes, and occasionally manages to do a load of laundry. Most of her writing (pre-COVID) was done in a pub where she could combine work with people-watching, a decent micro-brew, and a plate of Old Bay wings. This year, however, it's all about pajamas and the couch.

For more information:
libbyhowardbooks.com/

ALSO BY LIBBY HOWARD